PRAISE FOR *ULTIMATUM*

*"A heart-wrenching portrait of a dysfunctional family and its destructive force."

—*Publishers Weekly*, Starred Review

"Walton creates flawed, realistic characters that invite readers to root for them."

—*Kirkus Reviews*

"A powerful, big-hearted read."

—Anthony Breznican, author of *Brutal Youth* and senior writer at *Entertainment Weekly*

PRAISE FOR *CRACKED*

"In this powerful debut novel, K. M. Walton takes an unrelenting look at the corrosive effects of bullying, sometimes coming from where one would least expect it. *Cracked* crackles with emotional intensity from beginning to end."

—James Howe, bestselling author of *The Misfits*

"Readers who enjoy stories of dysfunction, personal growth, and redemption will love this book."

—*VOYA*

PRAISE FOR *EMPTY*

"Riveting, compelling, and brutally honest."

—Andrew Smith, award-winning author
of *Winger* and *Grasshopper Jungle*

"Like Walton's debut novel, *Cracked*, [*Empty*] wades fearlessly into the desperate inner lives of abused teens. Readers will feel Dell's pain acutely in this emotionally wrenching novel, which deals with serious issues."

—*Booklist*

"Teens will be sucked into [Dell's] downward spiral. *Empty* will hit home hard with teens who have been or are being tormented and should shed some light on how painful and destructive bullying is to its victims."

—*School Library Journal*

ultimatum

Also by K. M. Walton

Cracked

Empty

ultimatum

k. m. walton

Published by Sourcebooks Fire, an imprint of Sourcebooks, Inc.
P.O. Box 4410, Naperville, Illinois 60567-4410
(630) 961-3900
Fax: (630) 961-2168
sourcebooks.com

The Library of Congress has cataloged the hardcover edition as follows:

Names: Walton, K. M. (Kathleen M.), author.
Title: Ultimatum / K.M. Walton.
Description: Napervill, Illinois : Sourcebooks Fire, [2017] | Summary: When
    their mother dies, two very different brothers become even more distant,
    but when their father's alcoholism sends him into liver failure, the two
    boys must come face-to-face with their demons--and each other--if they are
    going to survive an uncertain future.
Identifiers: LCCN 2016016735 | (13 : alk. paper)
Subjects: | CYAC: Brothers--Fiction. | Death--Fiction. | Grief--Fiction. |
    Family problems--Fiction.
Classification: LCC PZ7.W1755 Ul 2017 | DDC [Fic]--dc23 LC record available at
    https://lccn.loc.gov/2016016735

Printed and bound in Canada.
MBP 10 9 8 7 6 5 4 3 2 1

To Christian and Jack:
I couldn't love you more. You are extraordinary
human beings, sons, and brothers.

OSCAR

I watch the nurse jab the needle into my father's arm. He doesn't make a move. He hasn't made a move on his own in days. I look over at my brother, Vance, and his head is down, lost in his phone. I close my eyes and just focus on breathing.

I feel a gentle squeeze on my shoulder. "That should make him comfortable, Oscar. I'll be right out in the hall if you need me," the nurse says.

Vance told me that since Dad had this thing called a living will with a do-not-resuscitate order, there are no IVs or breathing tubes or anything else that will help to keep him alive longer. His liver is in failure, *and* he doesn't have time to wait for a transplant. He will not be coming home from this place.

I nod. "Thank you," I say to the nurse. Why can't my brother put down his phone and be present?

"How long now?" I whisper. I read her name tag: Barbara.

She purses her lips into a tight smile. "I wish I could tell you. Definitely not today."

"Tomorrow?" This is the end of day two here at the hospice, and I've been told multiple times that he's not in pain, that they're doing everything they can to make him comfortable. But I'm not convinced. How do they *know* he's not in pain?

Barbara tilts her head and looks back at my comatose father. "Maybe, maybe not. He'll leave when he's ready."

I want to jump up and shake her. She's a damn hospice nurse! How can she not know? I want her to know.

I want her to tell me when he will die.

Sitting here watching him fail like this, so close, is harder than watching him live. I want it to just be over. I'm done.

"How many times does she have to tell you that she doesn't know?" Vance asks after she leaves.

I turn away and ignore my brother.

"I know you hear me," Vance says.

I lift my eyes and stare into his. To annoy him, I put in my earbuds and turn up the volume as loud as my phone allows. He shakes his head, indicating that he can hear the Mozart. *Good.*

My head fills with the layered richness of Symphony No. 29, and I let my eyes slide closed. While I'm into everything from baroque to classical to romantic, Mozart has always been my favorite. When I listen to his music, I'm taken out of my life.

My life right now consists of being trapped in this damn room with my brother and watching my father slip away one labored breath at a time. If I count the freckles on Dad's arm one more time, I may start drooling.

I steal a peek at Vance, and he's still glaring at me. When *isn't* he? Having Mozart drown out him and his never-ending dickhead ways is helping right now. I turn and gaze out the window.

Vance has never understood me—and he never will. Even down to the music I listen to. When we were in middle school, he'd make fun of me because of it. I can still see him playing an imaginary violin with wild, insulting movements, doing everything in his power to look weird.

Were Vance and I ever close? I blink and realize the answer. No, we've never been close—despite only being ten months apart.

I scroll back as far as I can remember, and my hands tighten into fists.

I think it's the classic "he took my place as the baby"

situation. Vance resents me—like, my very existence. He couldn't be any more unbrotherly. In fact, I'd say he stands firmly behind enemy lines. Let's just say that if I needed saving on the battlefield, Vance would probably let me bleed out.

My brother is an attention junkie, and apparently I robbed him of having our parents' complete and undivided focus. He has never verbalized this to me, of course—that would involve a deep conversation between us. This is all pure guesswork on my part. But I know I'm right.

VANCE

THREE YEARS AGO

"Turn up the music, Dad!" I shouted from the landing. "I can't hear it."

Reggae exploded from below, and I knew that would piss off my brother. I counted—one…two…three…door slam. Good. Let him hole up in his room scribbling shit in his sketchbook no one cared about. It was weird and he was weird.

I looked down at my homework and shoved everything into my backpack. I could do it on the bus. It wasn't right that my dad was down there partying alone.

When I walked by Oscar's closed door, I pounded on it as loudly as I could. I hoped I made his hand jump and he ruined whatever he was sketching. "Put your drawings down and play a sport, asshole," I shouted into the door crack. He didn't respond because he never had anything to say to me. Sometimes I wondered how we had the same parents. We were like peanut butter and onions.

Playing lacrosse was the best thing on earth. Who wouldn't like challenging themselves and being awesome at something? Every time I geared up and stepped onto the field, it motivated me to do better, play harder. Nothing beat the smile on Dad's face when I scored or took a guy out. Lacrosse made me friggin' happy.

Nothing made Oscar happy. All he did was mope around and make everyone around him miserable. With his grouchy attitude, he wouldn't survive eighth grade—and major bonus: I wouldn't have to be in the same school as him until my sophomore year.

I stood in the dining room and watched my father guzzle his can of beer as he danced around the kitchen. Something smelled good, and it was cooking on the stove. I glanced into the recycle bin as I walked to the fridge and did a quick count—nine empties already. My mom was going to freak.

I high-fived my father because the music was too loud to talk. I checked what was in the frying pan—some kind of chicken with mushrooms. He stumbled a bit and grabbed the counter. I ducked as he tossed his empty over my head and into the bin. By the time I turned back around, he was cracking open a fresh one. He was hitting it pretty hard for a random Wednesday night. Usually reggae-and-multi-beer dad didn't make an appearance till Friday night.

Suddenly, there was abrupt silence. My mother stood near the stove. She wasn't a fan of loud music. She grabbed the wooden spoon and stirred. "Is your homework done, Vance?"

"Yes," I lied.

"Where's your brother?"

I don't know why she continued to ask that question every day. She knew exactly where Oscar was. The same place. Doing the same stupid thing. "His room."

"Can you give your father and me a few minutes alone?"

Dad mumbled, "Whatever you have to say, Peggy, I'm not liss'ning." He defiantly drained the can and slammed it on the counter. "Turn the music back on, Vance."

She whipped her head around and looked me in the eye. "I need you to go upstairs now."

I took the steps two at a time, and that was the last time I ever saw my mother alive.

OSCAR

I UNFOLD THE CRISP, WHITE SHEETS AND MAKE UP THE pullout couch. My brother gets the reclining chair tonight—which means he has the horrible job of counting Dad's breaths till morning.

The nurse is here again. "Hey, guys, have you eaten dinner?"

Vance answers for us without lifting his eyes off his phone. "No, not yet."

"If you have money on you, I'd be happy to order something."

Vance ignores her as his fingers continue texting someone, most likely a girl.

I can't take my brother's rudeness so I speak up. "Yep, we've got cash. Thanks, Barbara. That would be great."

"Large pizza and fries good?" she asks.

"With sausage, and make it cheese fries," Vance shouts from my father's bedside without looking up.

I glare at him and wish I could make him disappear. "Thanks," I say to Barbara. She smiles this huge and lovely smile. Her cheeks lift, her eyes shine. It's been so long since I've seen a woman my mom's age smile like that. I want to capture it in a jar so I can study it. It's that perfect.

Barbara closes the door behind her, and it's just the three of us again. It's tiptoe quiet in the hospice. There are no beeping machines or IV wires in Dad's room, not like the ER. Here reminds me of the funeral parlor. Whispers, dim lights, sadness.

I leave my sheets till later and walk to my father's bedside. I assess him head to toe for the ten-thousandth time. He's still the color of mustard, and his hands and forearms remain blown up like balloons. His normally thick, wavy, dark-brown hair is now patchy and thin. I can see his scalp in many places.

Before he fell apart, whenever my father and I were together, everyone commented on how much I looked like him. I hate resembling someone I'm always so mad at.

My brother and I also share his stature—proudly described by my father himself as studly—which translates into tall, wide shouldered, small waisted, and naturally muscular.

Unfortunately, it's *my* facial features that are so similar to his. We've got the same full lips, big brown eyes, and wavy hair. Even our noses could pass for each other's. I know it infuriates Vance whenever someone says, "Wow, you can't deny this one," or, "He looks like you spit him out, Steve."

Vance looks like our mother: green eyes, straight, light-brown hair, and oval face. Truthfully, and I'd never tell my brother this, he's better looking than almost every guy at our school. But even his solid good looks can't extinguish the raging fire of jealousy he has about me being Dad's "twin." Trust me, I'd give almost anything to switch who we look like.

I continue studying our father. What bothers me the most is his mouth. It's wide open and just hanging there like he's surprised or shocked. Normally he's smiling and talking—not to me of course, to everyone else. His breath rattles in and out. It's the only sound sometimes for hours.

I lift the sheet and inspect his feet and calves. From the chair my brother huffs and chides, "I don't know why you keep checking underneath there."

The nurse explained it to us. But he probably wasn't listening, as usual. Barbara said they check the legs and feet for swelling, which means the kidneys are shutting down, which also means the person's body is that much closer to letting go.

I gently lay the sheet back down and stare at my father's head. Despite being propped up by a pile of pillows, it still dips at an inhuman angle, and I want to fix it. So badly. I begin what Vance has coined "rearranging his melon" and carefully move the pillow positions so that his head lies normally.

A long sigh escapes from his gaping mouth, and I startle. It's high pitched and resonant at the same time. It reminds me of a violin.

"What the hell was that?" Vance says. Obvious terror paints his face: bulging eyes, furrowed brow—the standards. Perhaps if he paid more attention to detail, he wouldn't be caught off guard so often. My brother lives for himself, lacrosse, partying, and girls. In that order. I fit into none of those categories, which means I don't fit into his life, and I never have. I figured this out a few years ago after our mother died. However, when I'm in bed staring at the ceiling, when the darkness is thick and blatant, I picture the time when I was six and Vance was seven, and he punched me in the stomach for picking a handful of dandelions for Dad.

I probably should've come to the conclusion then.

I place the pillow carefully next to my father's head. He has resumed his facial stance and is quiet. No more sighing. My heart slows down to a normal rhythm. I grab my sketchbook and pencil and take a seat on the overstuffed chair next to the pullout. I put my earbuds in but don't turn on music—I just want my brother to know I have no desire to talk to him.

Without Vance's knowledge, I begin sketching him and Dad. This book is filled with countless moments between them that I secretly captured, mostly at the Blue Mountain Lounge.

Dad named the bar he owned in town after the Blue Mountains in Jamaica. He and Vance were obsessed with reggae—just one more thing we didn't have in common. *I* was obsessed with drawing people. I'd draw him and Dad quickly, stealing glances when they weren't looking, adding details when I was back home in my room. Neither of them has ever laid eyes on my drawings. And they never will.

My sketchbook is for me. I express myself through my drawings without judgment. I don't need permission, there's no need for discussion—I can draw whatever I want. The sketches remind me that I'm alive, that I'm present. Here. That I exist. When my hand moves across the page, each stroke and smudge fuels me. It's as if the graphite has life-giving energy.

Without drawing and my music, I probably would've given up by now. I don't mean suicide or anything. I mean functioning like a somewhat normal human being. Drawing and music remind me that life has the power to be beautiful, that I just have to keep my eyes and ears open.

My brother disturbs my view when he leans in and rests

his forearms on the edge of the bed. He looks over at me. My earbuds must reassure him because he turns back to Dad and shouts, "Can you hear me, Dad? It's Vance. You gotta wake up, man. We leave for Jamaica in a few months. Seriously."

He is absolutely clueless. Dad already canceled that trip because of him.

VANCE

THREE YEARS AGO

Dad cried at Mom's wake last night. Shit, the whole funeral parlor practically dripped with tears. I was proud I kept it together. Shook hands with a million people and clenched my jaw tight each time. When my lacrosse team came through the line, I almost bit through my cheek. There was no way I was crying in front of those guys. Dead mother or not. No way.

Oscar had to be medicated like an old lady. Dad gave him one of Mom's anti-anxiety pills so he could function, and it turned him into a zombie. He blinked in slow motion all night, and all he could mumble was a weirdo version of

"Thank you." He sounded like one of the drunks at the Blue Mountain. He should've stayed locked in his room with his art and not stood there like a drugged psycho. Everyone I knew came through that line.

Each time I looked over at my mother's body, I swear to God I thought she was going to sit up, shoo everyone out of there, and send them on their way. I guess when you die at forty-eight—in a car accident that doesn't put a scratch on your face—you look that good as a dead person.

As if that made a difference. If one more person told me how beautiful she looked, I was prepared to punch them. Luckily, the last in line were two of Mom's old-lady coworkers and they didn't say it, or I would've laid them out right there on the cream carpet.

When the funeral parlor guy announced that tomorrow's burial information was being handed out at the door, the room cleared. He came back carrying a little silver tray with three Dixie cups sitting on it. He handed us each one, and I threw the ice-cold water back like a shot of vodka. I can't remember water tasting better than at that exact moment.

"You have anything a little stronger back there in your office, Bob?" my dad joked. Bob pursed his lips and shook his head. I was glad Bob wasn't standing as close to my dad as I was because his breath reeked of the two martinis he'd had for breakfast. Bob told us we could have a moment alone before they closed her casket.

I turned and stared at my dead mother. We'd argued over what dress to put her in. Each of us had a different favorite, a different moment attached to it. I wanted her to wear the dark-red one from the time we all dressed up as vampires for Halloween. It was Mom's idea, and I swear it was one of the only times we did something together, the four of us, and we had fun. Even Oscar.

Oscar wanted her to wear the orange-and-yellow-flowered sundress. He said it reminded him of sunsets. Dusk was her favorite time of day. She used to say how amazing it was the way the sky exploded in color, how it was so different from the bright blue of day. She loved how one thing could change so dramatically but still remain beautiful.

Dad's choice won though. She was laid out in her fancy, emerald-green lace dress. He said he loved it because it made her green eyes even greener, and she wore it whenever they went out to special-occasion dinners, otherwise known as the happy nights.

I got it. I understood. Dad wanted to remember her smiling and laughing. He wanted to remember her loving him. And she did love him, just probably a long time ago. I have memories from when I was little of them kissing and dancing

K. M. Walton

to reggae in the kitchen, of them being happy together. That all changed after Dad's first affair.

"I've stared at her enough today," my dad announced.

Oscar winced, knelt down in front of my mother's body, and dropped his head in his hands.

My dad threw his arm around me. "I need a stiff drink after all this."

"I hear ya, man. This was rough, Dad." He never hit the hard stuff. Beer was his thing. He said he hated the way some of his regulars at the Blue Mountain acted when they got into liquor. But Dad deserved to have as many as he needed. If there was ever a day for drinking, it was then.

"She shouldn't have stormed out of the house like that so mad." He reached up and pinched the bridge of his nose. "She never let me finish." That's when his tears came. He dropped his arm and turned away. I knew not to say anything. He needed to get it out. He'd been like a rock all night.

Dad was right. Mom shouldn't have left so angry. After I left the kitchen that day with the simmering chicken and mushrooms, my parents went at it. Screaming, crying, plate throwing. I sat on the closed toilet in the bathroom at the top of the stairs and listened to every word of their argument. It was where I always sat when they fought.

My dad had gotten caught cheating on my mother. Again.

This time it was with Miss Rawlins, Oscar's first-grade teacher. Dad must've run into her at the bar.

See, the thing was, I understood my dad. I got the impossibility of staying faithful to one girl. It wasn't supposed to be like that. Some guys weren't wired that way. He was a fan of variety and excitement. Truthfully, what real man wasn't?

My mother lost her shit that afternoon, and her voice hit levels I'd never heard a human voice reach before. My dad tried to explain that he was a man, and if she would take the time to understand him, things would be much better for her. She was real quiet at first, and it was a one-sided shout-fest, with my dad hurling slurred statement after slurred statement.

"You're too much. You get off on humiliating me, don't you, Steve?" my mother screamed.

I heard my father pop open a fresh beer, but he kept his mouth shut. I remember thinking, *Good call, Dad.*

"Alyce Rawlins?" My mother's voice cracked and she coughed. "She is young enough to be your damned daughter!"

When he told her Miss Alyce Rawlins—who was now married to Dr. Beech and known as Mrs. Beech—may be pregnant, the plates started shattering.

"I." *Plate smash.* "Am done." *Plate smash.* "With you." *Plate smash.* "Steve!"

He shouted, "Done? Where're you gonna go? I know everyone in this town, Peggy!"

"Then I'll move out of here. Vance will be getting his license soon."

Hearing my name being screamed from my mother's mouth made my stomach cramp up. My dad got Miss Rawlins pregnant? That sucked in every way something could suck. Everyone would know, and Dr. Beech was Oscar's orthodontist.

OSCAR

I CLOSE MY SKETCHBOOK AND STAND TO STRETCH. Movement outside catches my eye. It's the girls' softball team practicing on the side field. This hospice building is directly across from our high school, which is odd because in the three years I've gone to WCHS, I've never noticed this place. It was always just some medical building—one I passed day after day, completely unaware of the human lives ending, the wailing and hand-wringing taking place behind each window. I didn't know any of this world here existed, and I was better off for it.

Now I know.

My father's suite smells of grease and cheese, and my stomach is full of both. I shove my hands deep into my pockets and look for Jacque. I know she's out there so I squint to see if I can pinpoint her on the field. It's hard to tell the team apart—they all have baseball caps on. I think she's at bat, but I'm not sure.

Then she runs and I'm sure. It's her. No one runs as breathtakingly as Jacque Beaufort. It's like her muscles are conducting a magnificent symphony of movement just underneath her light-brown skin. It's stunning.

She's stunning.

And she doesn't know I exist. Well, technically, I'm pretty sure she knows I'm alive because she knows I'm Vance's little brother, but she's never uttered a single word to me. Not even hello.

The first time I saw her was when she walked in late to my sculpture class freshman year. She stood in the doorway looking flustered, tugging on her sleek, black ponytail and biting her lip. Mr. Gill ushered her in without any drama—he's the most laid-back teacher at WCHS—and she took a seat in the back. Right next to me.

Two days later, Jacque dropped out of sculpture, but in those two short days I learned all I could about her. She bobbed her right leg nonstop. The only makeup she wore was lip gloss. Her backpack was different from everyone else's—made of a coarse woven fabric with Rasta stripes and a drawstring. She never made eye contact with a single person in class because her gaze was always out the window.

We sat around tables in sculpture class so I had a full-on view of her face. Something outside captivated *her*, and it fascinated *me*. It was the way her eyebrows rose, the way her eyes danced, the way her mouth would slip into a tiny smile when she got lost in whatever she was staring at. Her expression was fleeting—but when you can't stop watching someone, you catch things. A few times I'd joined her and looked to where she did. It had to be the sky. There was nothing else to see.

My stomach flipped, wondering what made her light up like that. *Was* it the beautiful color blue? Was it her daydream? I'd eventually concluded—while simultaneously blanking out on what was going on in sculpture—that she felt things deeply. Like me. Clearly I had no proof of this conclusion, but either way, it started my crush.

A few weeks into freshman year, Jacque turned up in Vance's party photos on his Facebook page. That's when I realized she was in the popular group. My brother considers himself the king of WCHS, so if you're in a photograph with him, you're popular too.

Even though I suspected a girl that beautiful and emotionally complex was socially above me, seeing those Facebook photos is when I knew Jacque Beaufort was the princess to my peasant.

I continue watching the softball team do normal practice

things: throwing, catching, running, hitting. While behind me, roughly eight feet away, my father, my only living parent, has, according to the new nurse on duty named Marnie, less than forty-eight hours left on this earth.

I have an urge to smash through this second-story window without covering my face and let the shards of glass slice my skin, let the blood drip and drip and drip as I run across the field, grab the bat from Jacque's hand, and smash the world to smithereens. To the tiniest bits of nothing. Then perhaps we could all start over.

My father could be a sober businessman instead of a raging, alcoholic bar owner.

My mother could be his wife instead of his doormat. And she'd be alive.

My brother could be my brother instead of an inordinate blob of human skin that simply chooses not to understand me.

I could be happy. I could be free.

From behind, my brother says, "Why are you staring at them, psycho?"

I breathe in and I breathe out to clear the anger from my lungs. Why is he always so hotheaded? I ask myself this question multiple times a day.

I turn around and walk to my father's bedside. "I wasn't ogling the girls, Vance. I was simply looking out the window."

"Whatever. And can you stop talking like a dictionary? Talk normal." He rips off a piece of pizza crust and chews. "I wish I had a beer right now."

I squint. "The fact that our father is hours away from dying from liver failure has no effect on you?"

"Shut up! I haven't had a sip since my surgery. And if he was conscious, he'd be having one right now, *with* me."

Air shoots through my nose. "Well, you've certainly made the most obvious statement, now haven't you?" He goes back to watching the muted TV, and I go back to staring at our father.

Marnie comes through the door and stands with her hands on her wide hips. "How we doing in here, guys? How's the big man?"

"His breathing's still the same," I answer.

"I'm going to change his sheets and wipe him all down in about ten minutes. I wanted to give you boys some more time to finish your dinner."

"We're done," Vance says. He stands up and grabs his jacket. "I'm going for a walk."

"Good idea." Marnie nods. "Why don't you guys get the blood flowing while I get your dad situated?"

I know Vance wants to walk alone. I know I want to walk alone. Neither of us will verbalize this want of course, but we know what we want nonetheless. I grab my sweatshirt and let my brother disappear down the hall and around the corner. I make no effort to catch up or call out to him. I'd rather eat seashells.

As I saunter past the rolling nurse-station cart positioned directly outside my father's room, I hear a low, guttural moan from the room across the hall. I know I shouldn't, but I look in. An African American man is sitting in the recliner, obviously not the patient. He looks to be somewhere near my father's age—in his late forties—and he's the one moaning. It's like a cello, a rich and thick sound. I'm transfixed by it, and my feet are cemented to the carpet.

The man, who had just been running his hands over his bald head, drops his arms and they slap against his body. He looks directly into my eyes and we stare at each other, stranger to stranger. His mouth opens, and a fresh moan drifts out. I break eye contact and look at the occupied hospital bed. I can only see the lower half of the person. I have no idea the gender or age.

My feet have come back to life, and I walk quickly down the hall as another loud wail fills my head. The sound is weighted; I fear my skull will crack.

The man's pain is stuck to my skin. From the inside.

VANCE

TWO YEARS AGO

"Wake up! Dad puked in his bed," I shouted directly into my brother's ear.

Oscar rolled over and squinted. "What?"

I reached down and yanked the blanket off him. "Dad puked. Get up and help me."

We ran across the hall and stood at the foot of Dad's bed. My dad was covered in spaghetti-sauce puke, and the room smelled like a mixture of an Italian restaurant and the floor at the bar. "I'll roll him over to the one side, and you grab the sheets."

Oscar opened his mouth as if he had something to say but then closed it.

"What?"

"He'll get the mattress dirty."

"Yeah." I snorted. "'Cause he's not already covered in the shit or anything. It doesn't frigging matter." I tried to find the least puke-covered portion of his body, and there wasn't one. I ran into his bathroom and grabbed a towel. I wasn't a pussy, but I didn't want it on my hands. I rolled him once, and he didn't make a sound. Oscar reluctantly got to work removing the sheets from the one side. Then I rolled him back, and Oscar finished the job. "Wash them in—"

He cut me off. "Hot. I know. I've done this before."

We always let Dad sleep the day away and did our own things. Even though I was pretty sure he was done throwing up, I still rolled him onto his side. Just in case. He was the only parent I had left.

I heard the laundry going, and Oscar's classical bullshit music blared from his room. What fourteen-year-old dude listened to that?

I grabbed my lacrosse stick from my room and banged on his closed door with the handle. "Turn it down. You're gonna wake up Dad."

He turned it down, and I shook my head in the empty hallway.

OSCAR

As I step outside, my brother is nowhere in sight—and that sits fine with me. The early-spring air has a chill to it so I put on my sweatshirt. Each step I take puts distance between me and that moaning stranger's loss. I keep my eyes down as I walk. My sneakers crunch the shriveled brown leaves strewn on the pavement, left over from a recent spring pruning.

My life is in desperate need of pruning. I need the dead and withered to be snipped. I need to feel the bright-green shoots breaking through.

I come to a halt. *Listen to me. Using words that would infuriate Vance.* It's a habit I started in middle school soon after Mom died. I don't speak like that to anyone but him, and watching his reaction is really satisfying. He goes nuts.

As I walk, I wonder if the pruning event of my life will be my father's last breath.

The day of Dad's car accident we'd thought he was going to die in the ER. Turns out he stopped breathing and had to be resuscitated—the nurse told us after he was brought back. Surprisingly, that was the first time I'd looked my father's demise in the eye.

I remember saying to Vance, "What would we really do if Dad died? I mean, holy shit, Vance, what would we *do*?"

Vance's eyes bulged and he shrugged. "I have no frigging idea what we'd do."

My father dying, for real, just wasn't a reality for me. Despite Dad ramping up his drinking to vodka and scotch after we lost Mom and waking up covered in his own sick sometimes. Despite the ER doctor's warning about liver failure.

The curly-haired social worker talked with Vance and me as our unconscious father lay battered and bruised in his ER bed. She basically talked *at* us for about fifteen minutes. My brother had his glazed-over look on, so I forced myself to pay attention to what the woman said. She asked if Dad had a will. That question stopped Vance and me in our tracks. *A will?* A will meant dying. Death.

Once we calmed down, Vance surprised me by telling her that he did have one, actually two. A living will and a regular will. He said Dad showed him where they were and everything.

When she actually said the word *death*, Vance snapped out of it, strung a bunch of curses together, and flung them in the woman's direction. I remember her ducking down a little bit as he shouted.

He'd stormed out, and I apologized to her with sincerity. She drew the meeting to a close rather quickly. I had hundreds of questions floating in my head—the most pressing of which was, *Where would I live if my father died? With Vance? Alone?* But I didn't get the chance to ask her right then because my father had a heart attack behind the ER curtains. Every conceivable adult shifted into high gear, including the social worker woman. She yanked me out of the madness, found Vance, and deposited us in the waiting room. We were instructed to sit tight, which neither of us did once she was out of sight. Vance paced the length of the rectangular room, and I was up and down from my seat—getting drinks from the water fountain, going to the bathroom, grabbing a magazine, putting the magazine back. /

He didn't die that day. Obviously. He came to after the heart attack and then proceeded to shake uncontrollably, an apparent side effect from alcohol withdrawal.

That whole disaster was only two weeks ago, and my father

never regained full health. They'd kept him in the hospital for almost a week and sent him home to finish recovering. Each day he was home "recovering," he drank himself into a stupor. Last week, I noticed the yellow hue to his skin.

In retrospect, it was the beginning of the end.

VANCE

THAT TEACHER LADY DAD SLEPT WITH LAST YEAR NEVER was pregnant. Dad told me one night when he had a decent load on. The whole thing was a false alarm. When I lay in bed in the dark, I got bummed out that my mother died for nothing. I mean, her car crash was ruled an accident, but I knew better. The last thing I'd heard her scream at my dad was "I can't take this anymore, Steve. I want out!" Then our back door slammed, and the tires of her car squealed down the street.

I think she turned that steering wheel on purpose. She knew her car would crash into the tree. I was pretty sure my dad and my brother both thought the same thing. We never talked about shit like that though, so I guess I'll never know for sure if I was the only one.

I dropped my backpack on the floor of my dad's office and put on my apron. He was behind the bar taking inventory. "Yo!" I shouted to him from the doorway.

He looked up from the clipboard and tossed his head back in a silent hello. I grabbed the dolly and got to work loading it with cases of beer. As I finished stocking one of the coolers and turned to go load up again, I saw the half-empty glass sitting next to the cash register. My father's back was to me, so I leaned in and took a sniff. Straight vodka. "Hitting it hard today, huh?"

"How about you mind your own damn business! I had a headache," Dad barked. He never talked to me like that. What was with his crap moods lately? Maybe the hard alcohol was really messing him up. He swiped the glass off the counter, threw his head back, and drained the vodka. With a scrunched-up nose, he swallowed it down. "Haaaaaa."

"I've got practice in twenty, so Oscar's gonna have to finish this up."

Dad crossed his arms and swayed a little to the left. "Your mom never understood me." The sink underneath the bar was in the perfect place to steady him, and it did a great job of stopping him from falling completely over.

Okay. Wow. Random. I nodded because I agreed with him, but I had nothing to say, because what could I say to that?

"Remember that time we went to the zoo?" He didn't wait for me to answer. "We had a good day together. You guys got your faces painted, we went up in that zoo balloon thing, ate cheesesteaks by the elephants. Great day. Great *family* day."

I did remember that trip to the zoo, all of it, but none of what he'd just said made me understand his "your mom never understood me" comment.

He grabbed the rag and wiped the bar. "I like being a dad. I-I do. It's not easy for me, but I like it."

He *really* wasn't making any sense now.

"Your mom always wanted more from me. I never ever got it right, being her husband."

Why was he drunk-mumbling his feelings to me?

"Mom got so pissed at me that night when we got home from the zoo. She didn't like how I was talking to the cheese-steak girl. The cheesesteak girl! Who cares, right? She said I embarrassed her. I didn't mean to do that." He threw the rag into the sink. "Shit, I p-probably did. Live and learn."

Dad dropped his head and walked back to his office. That was some heavy, hard-to-follow shit. I grabbed the bottle of vodka and poured myself a shot. The front door was locked so there was no chance anyone would come in. I downed the shot and followed it with a second. It wouldn't be the first time I was buzzed at practice.

OSCAR

I SIT ON THE TOP ROW OF BLEACHERS AND STARE DOWN at the transformed football field. This time of year, the lines change location and shape, and it becomes our lacrosse field.

My brother's former paradise.

Unlike the softball field on the other side of school, this field is currently empty, as are the stands, so it's easy to determine that my brother isn't over here. It's just me and some middle-aged lady with a long, blond ponytail jogging around the track surrounding the field. My eyes bob along with her every step, and when she runs by the stands, I drop my gaze. She appears to be roughly the same age as my father. The same father who's about to leave his two sons alone in the world.

I abandon watching her and stare up at the sky, which

is turning itself into a postcard right before my eyes. The sun dips lower, and the magnificence of the slathered reds, oranges, and yellows makes me lost in the view. This time of day used to be my mom's favorite. Sometimes I'd join her in the backyard as she listened to reggae, sipping on a glass of wine, and we'd both gaze upward.

"So beautiful," she'd whisper and take my hand.

I'd squeeze my little fingers around hers and nod. Mom and I didn't need to talk. Even as a boy, I understood that she was appreciating the calm. I always hated when Vance would show up, bouncing around us asking a million questions about what we were doing, did I want to play tag, what was for dinner, what time was Dad getting home, and on and on until Mom would tire of answering him, kiss the top of my head, and say she was going to get dinner going. Vance always followed her inside, leaving me alone just as the sun disappeared. That absolute plunge into darkness was *my* favorite.

A few weeks before she died, I found her at dusk in the backyard, classic Marley coming from the outdoor speakers, wine in hand, and she quickly wiped her cheeks. I never asked her why she was crying. She took a sip and said, "Isn't it fascinating that the daytime sky is such a bright, clear, stunning blue, and then it changes to this?" She pointed up. "It's so completely different when the sun is going down. I love that."

"Transformation," I said.

"Exactly, Oscar." She leaned back in the patio chair. "Why is it that something as complex and huge as the sky can change itself every single day, yet people struggle against it so hard?"

I knew she was talking about Dad, but he was a mystery to me so I had no answer for her. Maybe she thought that if Dad could change—be better—then *everything* would be better.

"Your father used to make me laugh when I first met him. Did I ever tell you that before? He was so different from the guy I'd just broken up with. That other guy was so serious, so boring. God, your dad was fun. I wish we could have fun again." She drained her glass and then apologized for getting so personal.

"Mom, do you remember that trip we took to the zoo, the four of us? And Vance and I bugged you guys to let us get our faces painted?"

She smiled and looked away. She remembered.

"That was a great day. We could always go back there, to the zoo."

"I love that photograph we had taken of the four of us. So cute. We were happy." She goes to take a sip, but her glass is empty. "Your face was painted as a tiger, and Vance was what? A lizard?"

K. M. Walton

"A snake." I wanted to get the snake painted on my face, but Vance shoved in front of me and got it first.

"I just love that photograph."

Of course she did. It was the only framed family photo in our house. It sat prominently and alone on the corner table in our living room.

It seemed like she was holding back, that she had more to say, but she went inside to check on dinner, leaving me alone in the yard. The memory is depressing because I'll never really know. The only conclusions I can draw right now are: (1) I fiercely miss my mother and having someone want to talk to me like that. (2) It's time I get back to the hospice room. I've been out here for a while.

I walk across the street and am almost to the front door when I hear my name being called. It's Vance. Smoke escapes his cracked window. Great, he's getting high in the hospice parking lot.

His hand shoots out and motions me to his car. Before I make a move, I look around to see if anyone else is in the lot. It's not that I think my brother is motioning for someone else; it's that I'd rather ignore him than slink into his pot-filled car in front of watching eyes. I don't like assumptions. I do my best not to make them, and I definitely don't appreciate it when they're made about me. My brother and father have flat-out mastered the art of assumption. It's a trait I pride myself on not inheriting.

No one else is out here, so I walk to him. His window slides all the way down. Smoke billows out as if he himself were on fire.

"I thought you weren't allowed to smoke weed anymore," I say.

"Get in," he commands.

I make a face.

"It's serious. Get in."

The fact that our father may have died suddenly registers in my brain. "Is it Dad?"

"I'm not telling you shit until you get in." His window glides back up.

Control is important to my brother. Controlling me is even higher up on his list. I wish I could turn on my heel and leave him and his command to stew inside his smoke-filled car. In light of the situation, I do not storm off. I get in.

Vance squeezes the steering wheel. "His breathing is down to four breaths a minute."

"How do you know?" As soon as the question leaves my mouth, I feel stupid. He knows because he's already been back up there and the nurse must've told him exactly that. With an annoyed tone he confirms it.

"Did she say how much time he has left?" The answer to this question has become my personal obsession. I don't like surprises. I'm a planner, an organizer.

"A day, maybe less."

We stare out the windshield. A breeze blows through the trees. A red sports car drives by. We stare more.

Eventually I break the silence. "Do you think we should have Dad's will here?"

Vance huffs. "It's still in my backpack."

I wonder what Vance's reaction would be if I confessed to what I've been feeling in my heart—that I want Dad to die.

VANCE

TWO YEARS AGO

DAD MADE STEAK FAJITAS FOR DINNER. THE THREE OF US sat at the kitchen table building our meal, with Peter Tosh jamming from the speakers. Dad was a reggae fan as far back as I could remember. He said it started when he was in high school. One of his friends lent him a Bob Marley album, and that was all it took. He even got Mom into it. I think she started liking it on their honeymoon to Jamaica.

Reggae music was part of nearly every happy family memory I had. Like Mom vegging out in the backyard with a glass of wine, listening to Bob or Jimmy Cliff before Dad got home. I used to ask her a million questions, and she'd answer every one. She loved my questions. But that music was also playing in the background of my shittiest memories, like the night she died. Gotta take the good with the bad, I guess.

Speaking of "good," this was going to be a good dinner. A dinner like we used to have *before* Mom died.

Oscar said, "Can you pass the onions?"

I took a huge bite of my masterpiece.

The onions were next to Dad. He imitated Oscar in a high-pitched voice, "Can you pass me the onions?" The plate of onions stayed put. "You sound like a girl."

I swallowed my bite and looked up. I guess Dad was more shit-faced than I'd thought.

"Your voice sounds like a damn girl." He said it again. I watched him guzzle his glass of vodka and glare at Oscar. "Pass me the onions. Pass me the onions," he singsonged in his best girlie voice.

Oscar put his hands on his lap. My father reached down under the table, brought up the bottle of vodka that was wedged between his feet, and refilled his glass. Why couldn't my brother just ask again and make his voice deeper? What was the big deal? He was going to sit there and sulk like a pussy and ruin dinner.

My dad wiped his mouth off with the back of his hand. "How d'ja play today, Vance?" He was done with the girlie talk.

"Two goals. Garner's being a dick about passing to me though."

My dad ripped a huge burp and cleared his throat. "Be a dick back."

Before I could tell him that was exactly what I did, Oscar slid his chair away from the table and disappeared upstairs. His plate untouched. I reached over and grabbed his half-built fajita and piled on the missing onions. As I polished off the last bite, my dad leaned over to the iPod dock and cranked the reggae loud. He stood up and danced in the middle of the room.

My dad was having a one-man party, and it bummed me out. He should've been smiling, but he looked lonely and sad. *Shit, was he going to cry?*

"I love this song, Vance," he shouted. He sang along with Jimmy Cliff till the song ended. "Y-you know what? Do you know why I love reggae? Have I ever told you about the first time I cried from music?"

"No." *Dad cried from music? Did I want to hear this story?* Not that I would've stopped him, but I already knew why he loved reggae—it was its perfect mellow beat.

"Mom and I were on our honeymoon in Negril, sitting on the beach drinking rum punch. This three-man band was wandering around serenading couples. When they got to us, they broke into my favorite song. I-I didn't even have to ask them to play it. They just started singing Cliff's "Many Rivers to Cross." I remember looking over at your mom and being overwhelmed at how beautiful she was, how she l-loved me and married me, how lucky I was at that exact moment. Something came over me. It felt like a whoosh of, I don't know, happiness maybe. And I couldn't help it, I cried. It never happened again, that feeling." He spun around the kitchen, clapping his hands.

Dad stopped suddenly and leaned on the table, breathing heavily. "Oscar's just like your mother. So friggin' sensitive." The one-year anniversary of Mom's death was the next day, so maybe that was messing with him. He tossed his head back and forth. "So damn sensitive!" he shouted. He lost his grip and fell back onto his butt.

I jumped out of my seat. "Dad! Are you all right?"

He dropped his chin. "I-I messed everything up. Why do I always mess up? I miss her so much." When I went to help him stand, he smacked my hand away. "Leave me alone! You remind me of her too!"

OSCAR

VANCE WANTS TO FINISH SMOKING HIS BOWL, SO I gladly head in alone. The elevator ride up is brief but soothing. I've always liked the way my stomach feels floaty in my body. It's like a mini version of the roller-coaster sensation. That tiny bit of elevator pleasure lingers as I walk down the quiet hall— but ends when I look into the moaning guy's room. It's empty. The television dark. The shades pulled. The bed stripped.

He's gone, and so is the body he was holding vigil for. My eyes sweep back and forth as my brain tries to organize this new information. It's the sheetless bed that's getting to me. The way it signifies emptiness. The "once someone was here and now they're gone" feeling is so solid with the naked mattress staring at me.

I'm sad for this stranger and for his loss.

The nurse comes out of my father's room walking backward, talking to someone still in there. For a split second I wonder if she's talking to him. Maybe my father has rallied and beaten the odds…

A girl holding a laundry bag walks out, which confirms the fact that my father is indeed still dying. The girl and the nurse both turn and look at me. My stomach bottoms out.

The girl is Jacque Beaufort.

"Let me know if you need anything, Oscar," Marnie says as she takes her seat at the rolling nurse's station. "I'm sure your brother talked with you outside and filled you in, right?"

I nod. *What is Jacque doing here? How can she be standing in the doorway of my father's room? Wasn't she just at softball practice?*

"I changed your dad's sheets while you guys were out walking and talking."

Was Jacque in the room when she changed the sheets? *I've* been in the room when that happened and my father's hospital gown accidentally slid off, exposing him. Did Jacque see my father naked? My cheeks suddenly burn with humiliation. And the reason my father is dying is disgusting. He doesn't have cancer; he drank himself into a coma. This is none of her business.

I do not correct Marnie about her assumption that Vance

and I were out there "walking and talking," depending on each other, because the truth would be far too complicated to explain. Vance wouldn't walk and talk with me unless there was a loaded gun at his back.

Marnie says, "Oscar, let me introduce you to Jacque. She volunteers here for her senior class project."

Of all the students who could volunteer at the hospice, why did she have to be the one here? Today? Right now?

Jacque's gaze flicks away, and she shifts her stance. Looks like we're both very uncomfortable.

"She goes to WCHS too."

As if I didn't know this. I want to run away. This is the worst time in the history of time for me to meet her.

Jacque holds out her hand. "Hey, Little Irving. Oscar, right?" I'm stunned that she knows my name. My stomach flattens again. I blink and exhale. I should nod. *Should I nod?* Shit!

She drops her hand before I have a chance to grab it. I blew it. Now she thinks I'm rude like Vance.

For a split second we lock eyes—the light-blue color of hers is spectacular up close like this.

"I know your brother," she says.

My lips feel glued shut. I need to get away. I want to lock myself in Dad's room.

K. M. Walton

Her brows lift and her face lightens. She grins. It's the expression from our brief time in sculpture class. *Maybe I'm right. Maybe she is complex like me. Maybe—*

She says, "Okay, well, tell your brother I said hi."

Now I'm nodding.

She nods along with me. "And I'm really sorry about your dad."

VANCE

TWO YEARS AGO

At the bar, I finished unloading the last case of beer and clicked the freezer door shut. Oscar came barreling down the hall lost in his headphones, humming loudly. He didn't see me, and I took full advantage by plastering myself along the wall, waiting for him to pass, and then I jumped in front of him and gave him a pretty decent shove. His scream was so loud that Joey and Bill came running back.

"What are you two pricks doing back here?" Joey shouted. He hated when we goofed off. He was a bartender for life, and he took his job very, very seriously.

I was bent in half, laughing my ass off at the pitch of my

brother's scream. My father was right. He did sound like a girl.

Oscar was pink in the face, and I could tell he was pissed. *Whatever.* It was a joke.

"We're just messing around, Joey. No big deal," I said.

Bill shook his head and walked away. He never got as mad as Joey, but he probably just didn't give a rat's ass. Bill had only worked at the Blue Mountain Lounge for two years. He was always telling me how much he wanted to go to law school and that this job was strictly for putting money into his college fund. In other words, he was the polar opposite of Joey, who, I was pretty sure had never worked as anything else in his fifty-three years.

Joey yanked the white bar towel through his belt loop and shook his head. "You two act like a couple of kindergartners. No wonder your old man drinks so much."

Oscar's eyes bulged, and he went as red as a sports car. The way my dad partied made him all ragey, so Joey blaming him, even if he was just saying it offhandedly, was making Oscar furious. I could tell he was seconds from running away, like he always did. He never fought back. He never stood up for himself. His whole "run away and hide in my room" shit pissed *me* off.

"Did you finish unloading the beer, Vance?" Joey asked, his eyes squinted.

"Yeah."

"And you stacked it like I told you?"

"Yeah," I repeated with just as much annoyance.

"Why you gotta be such a prick?" he said.

I shrugged when I turned to leave. Oscar was gone. He was probably sulking in the alley behind the bar as usual. He would sit back there on that cruddy bench and do his homework. Or draw his stupid shit in that sketchbook. He was probably drawing sunsets and kittens. Or maybe the book was full of untalented chicken scratch. Who the eff knew what he had in there? He was so secretive about it, which was annoying.

I'd tried to get my hands on his book a few times, but he'd either be clutching it or it was in some hiding place I didn't know about. Yet.

OSCAR

Marnie escorts Jacque out. I overhear her greeting Vance. "Hey, Irving. That's your dad in there, right?" My brother must nod, because she says, "I'm really sorry. Let me know if I can do anything. I'm volunteering here for senior project, and today I'll be here till nine. So, if, like, your dad needs a blanket or if you want a soda...let me know."

"Thanks, Beaufort. This whole thing blows," he says.

She exhales loudly. "I can't even imagine. But everyone at school is thinking about you guys, even the teachers."

Their exchange is so natural, so easy. There are no bumpy parts, no uncomfortable silences. Confidence talking to Confidence. I'm jealous of how easy Vance's world is. Maybe emotionally skating above the surface simplifies things.

Regardless, Vance is still Vance, and I can tell he doesn't want to continue talking to her. She must not be on his hottie list. *This* part of his personality is so transparent to me, so crystal clear, the way he instantly compartmentalizes people into his predetermined categories. And if you don't fit into "buddy" or "someone he wants to have sex with," well, you are completely out of luck. You pretty much don't matter at all.

Brothers should matter to each other. Sons should matter to fathers. It's just how it's supposed to be. Even animals protect their young. I can't say that my mother truly understood me, but I knew she loved me and that was enough. She looked me in the eye and tried to figure out what was going on inside my heart. I always showed her my drawings, and she'd tell me I had a gift, that I should never stop capturing what I see on paper. Her words of encouragement never felt forced or fake. They were genuine and loving. They were music to my ears.

I sketched her the day before the accident. She was on the phone complaining about my dad to my aunt Renee. She had no idea I was drawing her. She cried when I showed it to her and hugged me for the longest time. She said I'd somehow managed to show her broken heart through her eyes. I'd only drawn what I saw. I had no idea that I'd done something so profound, so important for an artist.

I'd captured loneliness.

Long after her death, I concluded that loneliness was what connected me to my mother. We shared that hollow feeling, and she knew it.

My father linked on a guttural level with Vance. They spoke the same language, liked doing the same things, laughed at each other's jokes. I remember being on the baseball field, playing outfield, while my family sat just on the other side of the fence, watching. The ball was hit in my direction, but I didn't realize it because I was picking the grass and throwing it in the air and watching it cascade to the ground, so happy, so free. I wasn't paying attention. My head was not in the game, despite the countless catcalls coming from my father and brother.

Apparently, if I had caught that ball, my team wouldn't have lost. But I didn't catch the ball. It hit me on the forehead, so hard that I was knocked unconscious. I awoke to my father's voice. He was asking if I was all right, but it sounded more like he had to ask than like he really cared. There were people watching—the benches had emptied, and now everyone was huddled around me.

The look on my father's face, the not-so-hidden scorn, was so crystal clear to the eight-year-old me.

I couldn't control my tears, which repulsed my brother. He

said in front of everyone, "Stop crying, Oscar! It's your fault anyway." I knew he was trying to impress Dad. As usual.

My Little League career ended that season. So did me ever having a chance of receiving respect from my father and brother.

I think my fear of happiness sprouted during this time. Everything that brought me enjoyment made Dad and Vance angry. Being me seemed to irk them. So I did the only thing that felt normal: I retreated.

A little kid can only be scrutinized so many times by the two most important males in his life before things register in his brain, before he stops looking for acceptance. Before he stops expecting love and happiness.

Isolating myself obviously followed me into school. I know what people think about me there, people like Jacque. They think I'm quiet and weird and all wonder how I'm related to superstar Vance. No one messes with me, but no one makes an effort to hang out with me either. It's handy that I like being alone.

It didn't used to always be like this, the solitary thing. In elementary school, my brother's best friend, Stephen, used to include me whenever he was over at our house playing. Vance would eventually stop complaining and just let me play. He was never nice about it. It was more like he tolerated me to shut Stephen up. But when the three of us were laughing or racing or playing catch, I knew my brother and I were having fun. Together. I'd allow myself snippets of believing that Vance really wanted to play with me, that he did love me.

Everything changed once Vance and Stephen started middle school. It was like a switch got flipped. Vance nicknamed Stephen "Growler" because of some noise he made when he took his lacrosse shot. *Growler* wasn't mean to me or anything, but he stopped bugging Vance to include me.

It was the perfect recipe for me to duck and cover. I've been in that stance ever since.

Anyway, Jacque's popular. Her name is always mentioned on the announcements when they talk about softball. She obviously knows my brother, and she probably likes him. All the popular girls do. I wish I could warn them, tell them that he doesn't flush the toilet after using it, just so I'll find what he left. That he used to cry when he lost lacrosse games when he was little. That his room smells like rotten eggs and feet.

That he doesn't care, nor will he ever care, for anyone but himself.

But I don't because that's just not the kind of human being I am.

Vance enters my father's room. "Still four breaths?"

I look back to my father. "Yes." The sun is nearly down now, filling the room with streaks of marigold. "They did that radical change while we were out. I hate watching it, so I'm glad we weren't in here." I don't like the rag doll–ness of my father's body, the way his arms flap, the way his head has to be held so it doesn't roll around. He is everything he hated. My father is helpless.

Deep down, I feel a sudden spark of "serves him right." I turn away and try to squash it. It's too evil.

VANCE

TWO YEARS AGO

THE CLIP-ON BOW TIE WAS A GREAT DECISION. I QUICKLY adjusted it and ran my hand through my hair. I looked like a penguin, but when a hot junior girl asks you to prom and you're only a sophomore, you wore a tux whether you wanted to or not. WCHS did the combo prom thing—juniors *and* seniors. The whole lax team was going tonight, even Collin, and he was only a freshman. But he was a freshman who plays *varsity*, and lacrosse at our school was equal to football. If you were on either team you were at the top of the social pile. Like, the top-top.

Even though I was on top, I couldn't wait till it was over and we could party our faces off at the after-party. Dancing was stupid, and I hated smiling for pictures. Gwen kept saying that was the whole purpose of the prom. Since she had the best boobs, I figured I could take one for the team and slow dance a few times.

I pounded on the bathroom door. "I gotta pee. Get the hell out, Oscar!"

The door opened slowly, and I was face-to-face with my brother. He was almost taller than me, which pissed me off. His eyes swept up and down the length of me, ending with raised eyebrows. "Where's your boutonniere?"

"She hasn't given it to me yet, duh."

Oscar nodded and exhaled. "You look good, Vance." His eyes were locked onto mine. *Whatever.* I didn't need his approval.

Dad shouted from the base of the stairs, "Growler's here."

Oscar stepped aside and swept his arm out like he was allowing me into the bathroom. I wanted to smack the smart-ass grin from his face. I pushed past him and gave him a little shove.

Some nerdy chick from my gym class asked Oscar to this prom, but he turned her down. He didn't tell me. I overheard *her* telling her dork friend while we stretched our hammies on the mats. I could tell she was saying it kind of loud so that I'd hear. Everyone knows Oscar's my brother. Unfortunately.

I acted like I didn't hear anything and continued reaching

K. M. Walton

for my toes. Why he turned her down is unclear to me. Even though she wasn't someone I'd go for, she wasn't that bad. Pretty good body and nerd-genius smart, just like Oscar.

Well, I was glad he wasn't going. It would've ruined the night for me. He would've just sat in a corner and sucked the fun out of the entire room. Having him around was annoying, but mostly it was embarrassing. It would've been great if I had a brother who liked me and was into the same stuff. What did I get? Uh, *not* that.

I barreled down the steps. My dad, Oscar, and Growler stood near the door. "Don't get too plowed, buddy," my dad said. He grabbed my shoulder and squeezed.

"We won't, Mr. Irving," Growler said. "Just a good buzz."

Oscar crossed his arms and dropped his eyes.

"Too bad you're not coming, Oscar. You could've increased the IQ in our limo by a thousand percent," Growler said.

I squinted. What was Growler doing? Tonight wasn't about Oscar. Growler hadn't tried to rope him in with us for a long time.

Oscar's cheeks flushed. "I doubt it."

We had to leave before Growler made some stupid plea for Oscar to come.

My dad took a long swig of his beer. "The limo's at your date's house, Vance?"

I looked at the clock on the wall behind my brother. "Aw, man. We're gonna be late. And yes, the limo's at Gwen's. Waiting. They're gonna be pissed."

"Who cares? What, you think they'd leave without you two?" My dad shook his head and snorted. "You're the life of the party."

OSCAR

Growler stands in the open doorway. I refuse to call him Growler, mostly to annoy my brother. In my opinion, *Stephen* suits him much better.

He knocks on the open door. "Is this a bad time, guys?"

"You're kidding, right?" Vance smirks. "That's the dumbest question ever, Growler. Seriously? Yeah, this whole thing is a bad time. In fact, it's the worst fucking time I've ever had in my whole fucking life."

My mouth hangs open, probably wider than my father's. Doesn't Vance know that people have no clue what to do with suffering? With death? I'm not saying I'm, like, an expert on dying, but impending doom definitely increases insecurity. "He was just trying to be thoughtful, Vance.

Relax." I stand and offer my seat to Stephen. I can tell he's wildly uncomfortable about taking it. My chair is directly next to my father's head.

"No, no, dude. Sit down. I can't stay very long," Stephen says.

I nod and resume my position. "Well, thank you for coming."

"Are you kidding me? Visiting is the least I could do." Stephen smiles and shifts his stance. "My mom said that you guys are welcome to stay at our house, you know, if you need to."

Vance and I stare at him. My wheels are turning. So Stephen's mom is inviting us to live with them? I don't want to do that. Will we have to live with them when Dad dies? What if we can't stay in our house? I'm faced with a vast sea of overwhelming questions. My palms get moist.

Growler clears his throat. "So, how's he doing?"

Vance huffs. "He's dying. That's how he's doing."

I stand and say to Stephen, "Wanna come with me to get a soda?"

Stephen bobs his head.

I whisper to my brother, "He's here because he cares about you *and* Dad. Why can't you see that?"

"Shut the hell up! Don't tell me how I should feel. Isn't that what you're always shouting to me and Dad? Take a big

K. M. Walton

friggin' dose of your own medicine." Vance leans back in his chair, drops his head, and says, "Sorry, Growler."

"Stop, dude. No apology necessary." Stephen stands up. "It's all right. I know you're stressed out. I get it. Seriously, don't sweat it."

I motion Stephen out into the hall.

"Maybe I shouldn't have come," Stephen says to me. His eyes search mine for reassurance.

"He's been attacking everyone. He's even rude to the nurses. It's not you." I take in a huge breath, wipe my palms on my jeans, and look away. That's all I've got in me to let him know that coming was a really kind thing to do.

"It's okay. I'd probably be the same way."

My brow pinches. He'd never be the same way. Stephen's support was one of the main reasons I made it through my mother's wake and burial. He'd repeatedly checked on me, Vance, and my father. Besides the funeral home people, he was the only one who did. "You're not the same, *Stephen*."

He grins at hearing his real name, locks eyes with me, and nods. Maybe I've said too much. Stephen-Growler is Vance's friend, not mine.

VANCE

TWO YEARS AGO

WE ALL PASSED THE ENTRY BREATHALYZER TEST WITH flying colors. As soon as Growler and I walked into the gym, we ditched our dates and beelined to the bleachers. Being the genius best friend that he was, Growler had the idea to hide a water bottle filled with vodka that day after school. We made sure we used the same water brand the school used. Friggin' brilliant. We drained that sucker in three huge chugs each. I only gagged once. Then we popped two pieces of gum and went to get sodas.

By the time I found Gwen, I was totally buzzed. When I went to wrap my arms around her awesome bod, she shoved me away. "Ew. Really, Vance? You're drunk? How are you drunk?"

I couldn't explain because, yeah.

She glared at me like I'd killed her puppy and then stomped off with a bunch of her friends. I needed to sit down for a second. Just a second. My stomach was filled with booze. I could feel it sloshing around in there. Did I ever eat dinner? Shit. I should've eaten. I stumbled backward and plopped into a folding chair. Gwen was over in the corner surrounded by girls, like every girl in the world. They all kept looking at me. Where did Growler go? I squinted and scanned the dance floor. Fresh air. It was really hot in here. Fresh air. I wiped the back of my sweaty neck. I wanted to hang with my best friend. We planned this. Where was he? Maybe I should go splash my face with cold water. My eyes wouldn't stay open. What the hell? I only did four or five shots.

A couple lacrosse buddies were suddenly in front of me. Darren and Lucas. "Dude, you didn't share?" Darren asked. "Lame."

"Where's Growler?" I asked. My voice sounded far away. *What the hell?*

Lucas snorted. "What did you say?"

"Where's Growler?" I repeated.

"Are you stoned too? I can't understand you, dude," Lucas said.

Without warning, I had a guy underneath each arm and I was being told to "walk normal!"

"Where are we going?" I said.

"Don't talk, Vance. You're wasted. You're not making sense," Darren said in my ear. "Just shut up until we get to the bathroom."

My eyes refused to stay open, but I felt myself being sat down. Was I on the toilet?

Lucas grabbed my face and told me to open my eyes. "Just stay in here until you sober up. You'll get tossed out if a teacher sees you like this."

"Maybe we should take him outside," Darren said.

"What, so he can hurl all over a teacher on the way? Bad idea."

"We can't just leave him in here, Lucas. What if he falls off the toilet? Look, he can't even keep his body upright."

I felt myself lean to the side. Luckily the one stall wall was close, or I would've been on the tile floor. Everything swayed. I was a tree branch on a windy day. Ooh, Oscar would like that fancy talk. I gritted my teeth and tried to cement the thought to memory. I was the wind, right? Or was I the leaves?

"Shit!" Lucas shouted.

"Can we sneak him out somehow? There's gotta be a way to get him outside without the whole effing world seeing. Think, Lucas!" Darren demanded.

"I don't know! God, why do I have to solve this?"

"Is he passed out?" Darren asked.

Someone slapped me across the face, and I puked all over their legs.

OSCAR

JACQUE ROUNDS THE CORNER WITH A PILE OF BLANKETS in her arms. Her face lights up when she sees Stephen, and her pace quickens. "Hey, Growler."

Stephen shoots me a look. "Uh, Oscar's here too, Jacque." He points to me.

I'm used to being ignored, and the fact that Stephen has to stand up for me makes me sad.

She bobs her head. "Right. Sorry. Hi, Oscar."

I'm having the most difficult time concentrating. Her eyes seriously could be pools, which I know is such a cliché, but it's completely true. And the girl smells like lemonade. Honest to God, she smells like it. It's a breath of heaven in this hideous place.

"Can you hold on a second, Oscar?" She pulls Stephen a few feet away and whispers, "Their dad looks awful."

Even though she says it in a soft voice, I overhear. I cringe at her obvious statement. He's about twenty-four hours away from death—of course he's looked better. At least she's thoughtful enough to try and shield me from her thought.

Stephen nods and they walk back to me.

"Sorry," she says, wincing. "I should've pulled Growler farther away. I know you heard me."

Stephen draws in a huge breath and attempts to change the subject. "Did you do the stat homework yet? It sucks."

Jacque shifts the pile of blankets to her side. "Great," she deadpans. "I'm here till nine, and then I have to pick up my sister from ballet. All the way in Philly."

"Philly?" Stephen says. "Aren't there a bunch of dance places here in West Chester?"

She rolls her eyes. "She's a Level Three ballerina at the Pennsylvania Ballet. She's really good and all, but picking her up is a pain in my ass." A grin spreads across her face. "Wanna share that stat homework with me, Growler? I'll do the next one for us."

Stephen shrugs, and Jacque wraps her free arm around his shoulders.

"You are the man!" she exclaims.

Again I'm in awe of this effortless exchange, the way she threw her arm around him without hesitation. It all confirms my awkwardness.

Marnie appears at the end of the hall and shooshes her. She whisks Jacque away, telling her she's got blankets to deliver. Jacque turns and waves over her shoulder.

My stomach is in knots. Besides feeling crappy about my inability to interact with people, I am also pathetically superficial. I can't believe I'm allowing someone's looks and scent to affect me so deeply. If I was alone, I might have punched myself in the head. My lips tighten.

"I think you make her nervous," Stephen says.

I laugh because *that* is ridiculous. "Nervous? I don't think so."

Vance says from behind, "What the hell are you guys doing out here? Did you come to hang with me or not, Growler?"

VANCE

TWO YEARS AGO

I got buzzed every day of my suspension. All five of them. My dad let me work at the Blue Mountain instead of rotting in front of the TV at home. I took full advantage of the stocked bar every chance I got. Dad caught me once and told me to go easy. He didn't want me stacking the cases wrong. I did that last year when I was trashed, and he'd never let me live it down.

"Don't puke on those lemons, puke boy," Joey said, messing with me.

I held up the knife and stabbed the air.

"You gotta learn how to hold your liquor, son.

Throwing up on your buddies like that just ain't right," he continued.

I went back to cutting lemons for the bar. "Everyone pukes, Joey. They didn't care." *What was the big deal?* They did what they were supposed to do: help their teammate out. I can't believe I got suspended *because* of those two jackasses. I mean, they've seen drunk people before. But they both panicked when I hurled and ran to find a teacher. They said I was convulsing or some shit. I didn't believe it. Dad thought they pussied out and didn't know what to do with a little vomit.

All they should've done was make sure I didn't choke. Just like Oscar and I did with Dad. But no, they overreacted and got me caught.

Growler somehow managed to stay under the radar that night. He said he wasn't that wasted. I don't know how, because we drank the same amount of vodka. He must've eaten dinner. Not eating was definitely my downfall, a mistake I'll never make again. Live and learn, my dad always said.

Bill chimed in. "That's not what I heard." He snorted. "I'm friends with Darren's mom. Let's just say she got an earful about *you* from her son. He was less than happy with you."

"Darren hates his mom, so who cares what she says."

My dad came out of his office with his hands on his hips. "Who hates their mother?"

"My buddy Darren," I said.

He ripped a huge burp and rubbed his belly.

"Impressive," I said.

He bowed. "Women drive me to drink. And speaking of drinking, I need one." He poured himself a shot and tossed it back. "What time is it? Isn't Oscar supposed to be here by now?"

Joey shouted from the back, "Yeah, Steve. Oscar's definitely late. It's almost four."

My dad turned to me. "Has he texted you?"

I squished up my face. Oscar hasn't texted me since seventh grade. "No."

Dad pulled out his phone, read something, and did a facepalm. "Shit. His art show was today."

Joey leaned on the bar. "We'll take care of things here. Go!"

"No." My father shook his head. "It's over in two minutes. It was from two to four. Who runs a damn art show in the middle of the day? Doesn't that damn teacher know people work? Real jobs?"

"You hate art anyway, Dad." Lemon juice dripped down my arm right to the cut on my elbow. (I'd sliced it when I fell off the toilet.) I winced.

"True," my dad said. He mumbled curses under his breath as he walked back into his office and shut the door.

Oscar would be pissed and mope around for a few days, but he'd get over it. He always did.

OSCAR

I let Vance and Stephen sit in the mini–living room. I'm watching my father. Even though I'm counting his breaths, I crane my neck to eavesdrop on their conversation.

Stephen says, "Crazy that Jacque Beaufort works here, isn't it?"

"Yeah, sure," Vance says with an air of total boredom. "Are people asking where I am at school?"

"Everyone."

My brother must be smiling at that response. "Of course they are," he says. "That was a stupid question."

"I didn't mean to make you freak earlier." Stephen's voice is small. I can tell he's nervous. "I've never been in a place like this before. And it's awful seeing your dad like this. Is he in pain?"

Vance exhales loudly, and I wait for him to blow up again. "Nah, no pain. That's what a hospice is all about. They explained it to me and Oscar. They do everything they can to make the patient comfortable during their last days. No pain is what they do."

"How's Oscar doing?"

My brother has no idea how I'm doing. He remains focused solely on himself. As per usual. I lean over a bit, anticipating Vance's answer.

He huffs. "The fuck if I know."

At least he's honest.

"Coach told me to tell you that coming to a practice might do you good. Help clear your head. He said we're right across the street and you could be here in two minutes if you needed to be," Stephen says.

"Coach knows I can't do that. I don't *want* to."

They start talking about homework, and I zone out. I look down at our father with his slanted head, forever-open mouth. Hear his labored breaths. And I cry. The guilt over wanting him to die strangles me. It's hard to breathe. I try to let the tears flow as silently as I can, but they're clunky. I choke and then immediately cover it up with a fake cough. Having them hear me weep is the last thing I want.

My brother has always shown love and respect to this man

in front of me. He has idolized him and emulated him and, yes, he has loved him. I believe our father may be the only human being that Vance truly values. Dad is a prize to him. A hero. Even our mother never got the same treatment.

I love my father too. Children are programmed to love their parents. It's just how human beings are. So it's no surprise that the love I have for him is genuine. It's complicated, yes, but it's real. Last night, as I was falling asleep, I tried to think of something positive about me and Dad. I ended up with: college. One thing Dad believes in for me and Vance is going to college. Vance and I have known about our college funds since we were little kids. Dad never went, and it's something he's been passionate about for both of us.

College is the only topic of conversation where Dad and I can talk somewhat normally. Unfortunately, I can count those conversations on one hand.

With all that said, other than help pay for college, my father has done little to support me, to show me love, to care for me. To me, my father has been just as good as dead for my whole life.

I went inward after Mom died because I had no choice. There was no one left at home who valued my presence, who cared what I thought, who wanted to spend time with me. It was so easy to slide into my shell. Who would ever pull me out?

I choke on a sob and cover my mouth. I pretend to have another good cough to camouflage the crying, and I think it works. Vance and Stephen are lost in their own conversation.

I'm just plain lost.

VANCE

TWO YEARS AGO

My dad had disappointed me, yeah, but what parent hadn't let their kid down at some point? He'd missed a few of my big games, but I'd never cried about it or made him feel bad. He wasn't perfect. Who was? So when Oscar refused to speak to him for, like, a week after Dad missed his art show, I was fired up. I told him he was being a selfish baby and that Dad could see his stupid paintings or pieces or whatever-the-hell he called them if he just brought them home.

Oscar ignored me, of course.

I swear he didn't eat with us for days and days. He went straight to his room after school and didn't come out till morning. I have no idea what he ate, or if he ate at all. If he was looking for pity, he would get none from me. People forget shit all the time. Who did he think he was? The king of the world?

Dad was usually clueless about emotional stuff. That was Mom's job. She'd go talk to Oscar. I don't know what she said to him, but he always came out of his room happier. Now she was gone, so no one went to talk to Oscar.

Dad acted like everything was totally normal. He made dinner, set a place for Oscar, called him down. Nothing. We'd be jamming to reggae. We'd eat dinner. Tell stories. Regular stuff.

This went on for a while. Then one night Oscar just showed up at the table, as silent and moody as ever. I opened with a jab, "Look who decided to grace us with his presence tonight," and I got the evil eye from Dad. That didn't stop me. "No, Dad, he needs to grow up and realize the world doesn't revolve around him and his little drawings. You were working. You weren't out partying. Wor-king."

Oscar stood up and walked upstairs. We didn't see him at the table for another week.

The baby.

I'd admit it: I liked not having Oscar around so much. He had a knack for annoying Dad with his high-and-mighty crap, which was something I rarely did. Dad and I spoke the same language. Oscar was like an alien.

While Oscar was sulking in his room all those nights, Dad and I had tons of time to talk lacrosse strategy and music, shit my brother didn't care about. We jammed to tunes as loud as we wanted. He said I could go to the upcoming Reggae Sunsplash concert at the Mann, said he'd drive me and Growler *and* pay for me if I scored a hat trick in my next game. I took the challenge.

It would be great to get stoned out of our minds, listen to Jimmy Cliff and Toots and the Maytals, and not have to worry about driving home.

Perfection.

See, Oscar didn't even know what he was missing. If he would stop being such a whiner, he could actually have a life.

OSCAR

Stephen's gone, and my brother and I flank our father's bed. My gaze is locked on Dad's chest, counting the breaths. Vance is playing some game on his phone.

Still four breaths a minute.

Without looking up, Vance asks, "Still four?"

I nod, knowing my answer won't register. Passive aggression at its finest.

He asks again.

I nod again.

He stares at me. "What's your problem?"

A fresh wave of guilt washes over me. Now's not the time for me to be a dick. "Sorry. Yes. Still four."

Vance huffs and bites the inside of his lip, something he

only does when he's worried, which doesn't happen that often.

"What time is it?" he asks.

Instead of snarking that he's got his phone right in front of him, I say, "Almost nine." I yawn and start a new breath count. My heartbeat doubles. I think I just counted three breaths. *No, count again.*

One.

Two.

Three.

Shit.

"Vance, he's down to three breaths."

My brother pops up, his phone clattering to the floor. "What?"

"Look," I say. We count and time. "Three."

He runs from the room, and within a few seconds Marnie is back with him. Her lips tighten, and she squeezes my shoulder.

"Is it happening?" I whisper.

"Let me see how he's doing first. Okay?" She feels his forehead, lifts the covers to survey his legs and feet, and starts her own breath count. "It *is* three, guys."

This is real. *My* lip quivers so I bite it. I've been secretly wanting it to happen, but now that it's so close I...I...

Oh God.

Vance's face drains of color. "He's never opening his eyes again, is he?"

Marnie turns to Vance and takes his hand. "Aw, honey. I'm sorry. No. We've done everything we can to make him comfortable."

Vance says, "What Oscar said. Is it happening?"

"All I can tell you is that he's closer to passing, but I can't tell you for sure that it's going to happen tonight. We do see a lot of patients let go while their loved ones are sound asleep, almost as if they're sparing them from the last goodbye. Some wait until family members are all here. Everyone is different."

Neither of us have a response. We both simply stare at her.

"Oh, boys, I'm so sorry. This is a tough situation. You're going to have to dig deep and be strong."

I guess Marnie is forgetting that we've already lost our mother, so we're intimately familiar with digging deep.

Marnie steps back and says, "If there's anybody you'd like to call, to let them say their goodbyes, I'd do it. Just let me know their names so I can let the guard downstairs know and he'll let them up."

"We should call Joey and Bill," I say.

Vance nods. "I'll do it."

"Uncles?" Marnie asks.

"No. They're my father's bartenders at the Blue Mountain,"

I say. My father is an only child. Both of his parents died when he was in college, and my mother only has one sister who lives in Singapore. I turn to Vance. "What about Mom-Mom and Pop-Pop?" They're my mother's parents who live in Alaska. Yeah, Alaska. And even though we've only seen them a handful of times throughout our lives, they should probably know that their son-in-law is about to die.

My mom shared her regret with me about losing touch with her parents during one of our last "in the backyard, listening to reggae, looking at the sky" moments. She admitted to missing them, which is something I'd never heard her say before. It was no secret that Mom-Mom and Pop-Pop resented Dad for taking their daughter so far away. They were also not fans of his infidelities. Go figure. Throughout my childhood, I'd overheard lots of telephone arguments between Mom and her parents, and she was always so protective of Dad. It used to make me angry. I wanted her to tell them the truth—that she was in love with a guy who didn't know how to love her back.

She never did patch things up with them.

Vance says, "You seriously think they'd care? They didn't even come to Mom's funeral." He shakes his head. "I mean, Mom was their *daughter* and they didn't come. So they're definitely not jumping on a plane to come be with us, that's for sure. So what's the point? I don't think they even know our names, for fuck's sake. The last time we saw them, I was seven."

Marnie clears her throat. "I'll let you guys hash this out privately. So you want Joey and Bill on the list, right?"

"Yes," we say in unison.

Vance is right. They'd never come. They hate Dad. Quite frankly, I hate *them*. How do parents not come to their daughter's funeral? "I agree with you, Vance."

He tilts his head. "What?"

I quietly snort. This may be the first time in our lives that I've said those words in that order to my brother: *I agree with you, Vance.* "I said I agree with you. Mom-Mom and Pop-Pop *are* assholes. There's no way they'd care about Dad. They don't deserve to be told."

Vance's brows shoot up, and he looks from side to side. "*Me?* You agree with *me?*" He turns and peeks out the window. "Is it snowing outside?" He smiles and then scrunches his nose. "They are assholes, aren't they?"

This feels right, us both calling our grandparents a-holes, and that is strangely perfect.

VANCE

TWO YEARS AGO

"Where's your dad?" Growler asked and handed me the glass bowl.

I shrugged, took a hit, and lay back down. Concerts at the Mann Center for the Performing Arts meant bringing blankets, staring at the nighttime sky, and of course, smoking weed. I hadn't seen my dad and his buddy Tom since we parted ways at the entrance. My dad knew we both needed our space to party.

"Pressure Drop" started from the stage. "Sweeeet," I said. That was my favorite Toots song. I wanted to dance. Screw vegging out. I hopped up and jumped around as much as I could. It was sandwich city out there on the lawn, and blankets were everywhere. But a reggae crowd was usually pretty chill.

The song ended and the band left the stage. Jimmy Cliff was next, my dad's favorite. It would've been cool for us to hear him together. I kind of wished I knew where Dad was. I looked around, but, yeah, too many people.

"Vance!" someone shouted from behind.

I turned and saw a sea of bodies.

"Over here! Vance!" It was a girl, and her voice was a little closer.

I looked to my right to see Jacque Beaufort jumping up and down, waving her arms. I waved back. "Dude, Beaufort's over there having a cow," I said to Growler.

He remained sprawled out on the blanket. His arm shot up and he waved. "Cool. That's cool." He was as high as a kite.

She and three of her friends made their way to us. "Hey. How great were Toots and the Maytals? Right?" Jacque said.

Damn, her eyes were friggin' blue. But she wasn't my type. Her hair was too dark. I was pretty sure she was half black or something. I liked blonds.

Jacque checked out who was on our blanket. "Just you two?"

"Lucas is here with his girlfriend. We never found each other though."

She nodded. "Your dad's gotta be here."

Because of the Blue Mountain, everyone in town knew my dad was into reggae. Weekends he'd bring in no-name reggae or ska bands from Philly or New York, and he'd pack the place. West Chester, Pennsylvania, wasn't exactly tropical, but anyone who came into the Blue Mountain Lounge sure got a taste of Jamaica. I smirked. "Yeah, he's here somewhere."

"Cool," she said. "My parents are here too. My mom's from Montpelier, near Montego Bay. She knows Jimmy Cliff's cousin."

So Jacque *was* half black. I knew it. I blurted out, "Does she know any Marleys?"

Her blond friend giggled. She stood in a shadow so I couldn't see her face, but she had a hot body.

They all looked at Jacque and she grinned. "Everyone from Jamaica knows a Marley."

"So you've been there?" I asked and immediately felt like an idiot. Of course she'd been there. She just said her mother was Jamaican.

Her eyes lit up. "Oh yeah, at least twice a year. You?"

"My dad said he's gonna take us there after I graduate."

"Cool." She rocked on her heels. I could tell she wanted to say something else. Shit, I hoped she didn't come on to me. I was too high to think of a subtle brush-off.

Jacque looked away. "Little Irving here too?"

"Oscar? Are you shitting me? He's probably home jacking off to some Beethoven song."

The blond stepped forward, moonlight hitting her face, and she yanked on Jacque's arm. "You didn't introduce me."

Whoa, wow, she's absolutely beautiful. Brown eyes and a great smile.

Jacque smacked her own forehead. "Right, sorry. Vance, this is my friend Christina. She goes to Archbishop Wood. Our moms have been friends since college."

Christina held out her hand and I stood frozen, staring at her face. She playfully touched my shoulders and shook me. "Where did *you* just go?"

I tossed my head back and laughed. "I'm pretty baked up. Nice to meet you." This time I offered my hand and she took it. Her grasp was warm and firm, and I wanted to pull her into my arms and just make out.

But I didn't because that would've been completely uncool.

Christina leaned in and whispered, "Easy, killer, I have a boyfriend."

Of course she had a boyfriend. *Was I imagining her flirting? How high am I?*

My face felt hot. Thank God for nighttime. I whispered my response, "Relax, Chrissy. You're not my type." Even though that was a bullshit lie, it felt good to zing her back.

She pulled away and smirked. "Let's go, Jacque. I have to use the bathroom."

"Later, dudes." Jacque nudged Growler's foot as a goodbye.

He shouted long after they were gone, "You guys have any snacks on you? I'm wicked hungry." He was in his own world down there.

I'd have given anything for a container of nachos or Christina's number.

OSCAR

I listen as Vance calls Joey and Bill. His voice cracks with each brief conversation, and both times he shoots a look over his shoulder to see if I'm listening. I pretend I'm not, but I am.

"They're both on their way," he says. Vance plops down hard into the leather reclining chair and slams it back, his legs snapping up with the footrest. He punches the armrest a few times and looks out the window. There's nothing to see except a streetlight and a tree. It's pitch-dark outside.

"What about Aunt Renee? I mean, I know she's not going to fly all the way from Singapore or anything, but she does know Dad," I say. "I'll—"

Vance cuts me off. "Sure. I guess. But I'm done calling people. If you want to call people, go ahead."

If he'd let me finish, I was about to offer that *I'd* call her. I didn't want to stress out Vance any more so I let it go. As I turn on my phone, it dawns on me that I don't know her phone number. The one aunt I have, and I don't have any way to contact her. A frustrated sigh slips out.

Vance turns his head. "What?"

"Do you have her phone number?" I know this is a ridiculous question. Vance having Aunt Renee's phone number would mean that he has called or will call Aunt Renee, and that simply isn't true.

"Why would I have—?"

I cut him off. "Where's Dad's cell? He's gotta have it."

"We don't know his password, remember?"

Vance is right. We already tried everything we could think of, and our cell provider won't give us the code until our father is dead. (Isn't that nice?)

"I wonder if Mom has the number in her old address book," I mutter to myself.

"Aunt Renee didn't move to Singapore until *after* Mom's accident. Her current number wouldn't be in there. Remember?" Vance's tone drips with annoyance. He should be sitting in a puddle.

"All right, Vance. I got it."

I guess we're not calling Aunt Renee then.

I take a seat in our sitting area and put my feet up on the coffee table. "Stephen left his sunglasses here." I hold them up for my brother to see.

He doesn't lift his head or open his eyes. "Mmm-hmm."

I fold them up and place them on top of the dresser. When I resume my position on the sofa, it hits me: I don't have anyone I want to call about my father's looming death. There are people I talk to in my classes—people who are nice to me and to whom I return the niceness—but I'm a loner. It's not something I worry about; it's just me. Being by myself brings me peace. I'm not a people person.

After Growler pulled away and stopped including me, I spent a lot of time alone, and I liked it. It felt good for me to have my own space.

Besides, no one's into what I'm into, so I've found it useless to try to include people in my world. I know this sounds like I'm a complete weirdo, but I'm not. Like I said, I'm just me, and I'm fine with that.

Why am I caring that I don't want to call anyone? What would having someone here actually do for me? I'd have to make small talk and worry about what they're thinking—two things I'm not capable of right now. I can barely concentrate on one thing for more than a few minutes. Having people from school visit would be nothing but a hassle.

I look at Stephen's sunglasses. I stare long and hard at them.

Stephen is practically part of our family. He and Vance became really close after Mom's funeral. He slept at our house more than he slept at his own in the months after she died. Vance rode me less when Stephen was over. That's probably why I like the guy so much.

But he's Vance's friend, not mine. And believe me, my brother never lets me forget it. He treats Growler like a brother. When he gets a glass of ice water, he makes one for Growler without being asked. They have lacrosse tosses in our backyard, sometimes for hours. They sit shoulder to shoulder and laugh at Vines. They stay up late watching old episodes of *SpongeBob*, laughing and saying lines along with the characters. There's conversation. There's understanding. There's trust and fun and happiness.

There's everything I should have with Vance.

VANCE

TWO YEARS AGO

GROWLER AND I GOT ESCORTED OUT OF THE MANN. THE guard said he had to lock the gate. We'd searched for my dad and Tom for over an hour. Tom had met us there so he was probably long gone.

"Do you think my dad got a ride home with Tom?" I asked Growler.

He huffed. "Shit, I don't know. Maybe."

"Wait, if he did, that would suck. My dad has the keys, dude." My high had worn off, and I was close to flipping out.

"Should I call my mom?" Growler asked.

"No! Shit. She'll freak." His mom almost didn't let him

come, and the only reason she gave in was because a parent would be with us.

The parking lot was dotted with a handful of cars; the crowds were long gone. My dad's SUV was still there. I was hoping he'd be sitting in the car waiting for us, but the car was dark.

"Call him again," Growler suggested.

I tapped in Dad's name, and my phone rang until his voice mail came on. I didn't leave a message that time. "Voice mail."

"Do you think we should call the police?"

"The police? Holy crap, Growler, what the hell do you think happened?"

He winced. "I don't know, but it's after midnight and we can't find them. He hasn't answered his phone all night. What if he can't answer? You know?"

My head spun. My father was fine. He wasn't in trouble. There was no way. He was fine. "Shut the fuck up, Growler. Okay? Just shut the fuck up."

He did.

Over the next twenty minutes I called Dad's phone ten times, all with the same frustrating result. When the workers and guards started coming out to their cars, I suggested that we hide in the woods next to the lot. I didn't want anyone asking questions.

From behind a huge tree, Growler and I watched the last employee leave. The lights inside the Mann dimmed and faded to black. Luckily, the parking lot remained bright.

"I need to get home, man," Growler said. "My mom has already texted me twice. I told her we stopped to get food and it's taking forever. I can't hold her off much longer."

I held up a finger to make him stop talking, and I called home. Oscar was there. He would answer. Maybe Dad *was* home. Oscar picked up after five rings. "Hello?"

"It's Vance. Listen. Is Dad home?"

"What?"

"Go check if Dad's in his bed!" I barked.

I heard his bed creak as he sat up. He huffed in my ear as he made his way to Dad's room. "Not here."

"Shit," I mumbled to myself. "I can't find Dad. Check your phone. Did he call you tonight?"

"Wait, Dad is missing?"

"Asshole, yes, I just told you that. Did he call or not?"

Oscar exhaled loudly. "I was just sound asleep, Vance. Don't get mad at me."

I screamed, "Did Dad call or not?"

"No." And then he hung up on me.

I pulled my phone away and glared at it.

"What did he say?" Growler shouted.

"Nothing! He hung up on me."

Growler shook his head. "Well, you called him an asshole. So…"

My phone lit up and rang. It was a call from home. Maybe Dad just got dropped off by his buddy, and he left his keys for us somewhere. "Dad?"

"No. Now shut up and listen to me. Dad is probably passed out somewhere on the property. You two have to go look for him," Oscar said.

"You shut up and listen to *me*. Growler and I already searched the whole effing place. Twice. Got any other brilliant ideas?"

We breathed into each other's ears.

He whispered, "I'm scared, Vance."

What? He's *scared*? How frigging annoying could he be? Why should I comfort him? I was stuck out there; he was home. "Shut up! You're so selfish. This isn't about you. *I'm* the one here! Why can't you help me for once? Why do you always get to be the baby?"

And then *I* hung up on *him*.

OSCAR

"Hey, guys," Joey says. Bill stands next to him. They both look about as uncomfortable as any two men could look. Neither of them makes a move to come in. They are frozen in the doorway.

When Vance doesn't greet them, I pop up off the couch and usher them in. I'm about to tell my brother how rude he is, but he's sound asleep in the recliner.

Bill and Joey exchange a nervous look. Bill whispers, "Should we come back later?"

Joey has his eyes fixed on my father, clear shock registering all over his face. He shakes his head. "No, Bill, there won't be a later." He smacks Bill's arm.

"Aw, hell," Bill says.

The three of us stare at my father's face for quite a while. No one speaks. We all just gaze upon the face of death before us.

Joey clears his throat. "My grandpop had that same face. Damn, I remember it."

Bill bites his nails, a habit he's had since the day I met him. "They're sure he isn't going to wake up? I mean, he's a real strong guy. I saw him level a drunk guy who was pushing his wife around at the lounge just last year. Dropped him in one punch."

I don't want him to wake up.

I wince at my thought. It's the worst thought a son could have about his father. My hands tighten into fists. The reasons and memories behind my feelings are many and painful. Watching Dad sink deeper and deeper into alcoholism after Mom's death wasn't easy.

Vance yawns and says hello. Everyone is drained. Everyone is lost.

I ask if they'd like some privacy to say goodbye. Both men's eyes go glassy with pain. They nod, and Vance and I walk to the Common Room in silence. The Common Room is actually a large living-room-type room with overstuffed sofas, two recliners, a huge dining room table and chairs, built-in bookshelves made of dark wood and filled with hundreds of books, fresh flowers on every table, massive framed photographs of various beaches, and a shiny black piano. I've never sat in the room, only passed it on my way out.

We each take a sofa and sit. In silence.

Marnie appears with her gentle smile and big blue eyes. "Either of you play the piano?"

Vance shakes his head, and I'm about to do the same when he says, "He used to."

"Ooh, honey, play something. Everyone loves it when we have a player on the floor. We all swear it brings peace to the patients."

I shift in my seat and give Vance the death stare before speaking. "I haven't played since fourth grade. I'm sorry."

She puts her hands on her hips. "Oh, come on. I'll bet if you sat down and tried, it'd all come back to you. We don't care if you play 'Mary Had a Little Lamb.' We just like it when this thing gets used." She pats the top of the piano. "Go on, give it a go. Trust me, no one will notice if you hit the wrong keys." A grin spreads across her face.

Vance is lost in his phone so he doesn't give a damn one way or the other. I purse my lips and rack my brain for a song I could play.

"There's a bunch of piano books in the bench," she says.

She's being so nice to me. I stand up and walk over.

Marnie's got the bench open, and she's rustling through the books. "People donated these. All those too." She points to the shelves lining the wall behind me.

My stomach flips when I spot a familiar cover on one of the piano books. It's the Bela Bartok book my old piano teacher, Mrs. Gramble, used during my last year of lessons. Not *the* book, but a book exactly like it. I pick it up and thumb through the pages. "It's even Volume Two," I say to myself.

"You know it?" Marnie's eyebrows raise in anticipation.

"Yes, but I don't think I remember how to play anything. Practicing wasn't exactly my thing."

Mrs. Gramble introduced me to classical music in first grade, and it was unintentional. It happened in the hall outside her studio office. My mother would drop me off, and I'd sit out there clutching my *Hal Leonard Easiest Piano Course* book and listen to the music coming from a small CD player underneath one of the chairs.

The first time, I found the music kind of scary. I'd never heard anything like it. But the second time, it seeped into my little six-year-old soul. I ended up moving to the seat directly over the CD player. I remember wanting to get closer to the sound. When, months into our lessons, Mrs. Gramble found me lying on the floor with my head underneath her chair and my ear pressed up against the speaker, she was startled at first, but then she knew. She knew I'd fallen in love with the music.

Poor Mrs. Gramble tried to teach me how to become a classical pianist for three out of the four years. It didn't work. She blamed my slow finger movement, but I knew it was because I never practiced. Ever. I only wanted to hear the music, not play it, apparently.

However, the music became deeply personal to me. Part of my identity. The concertos, requiems, and symphonies grew roots inside me. The music was where I went—where I go—when I needed to put myself back together. Note by note. Especially when I was drawing. It was as if the music itself breathed life into my sketches, each lift and sway of the instruments, each bit of intensity or gentleness guided my hands. Those moments brought me happiness.

I stop flipping pages. No. 38. Winter Solstice Song (Molto vivace) stares back up at me.

Marnie says, "Go on. Give it a go."

I try another angle to get out of it. "But it's almost nine. Won't that disturb people?"

"Honey, trust me. When music fills these halls, the darkness lifts."

I wish I could run through it a few times in a private space, just so I could work out the kinks and not sound like a mess.

Who am I kidding?

This one piece I could play with my eyes closed. It's the only one I ever truly liked in my four years of lessons. The one that came so naturally while learning to play it that it frightened me a little—it was as if I'd already known where my fingers should go.

It was the only one that ever made me cry.

It was my secret. I never even told Mrs. Gramble. During my lessons I'd intentionally mess up and have to start over. I tested that woman's patience weekly.

In fourth grade I was two years into my "let's keep things that make Oscar happy a secret" way of thinking. I didn't want my father or Vance to know how that song made me feel, how it was practically a part of me. My stomach would knot each time I pictured either of them finding out. They would find a way to ruin it. I knew they would.

Marnie gives me a little nod and a smile. I look over to Vance. He's gone. Maybe he went for another walk. My stomach flips with relief. Playing in front of him is the last thing I want to do. My brother is a contributing factor in why I chose to stop playing.

He had a lacrosse practice at the same time as my fourth grade recital. At first my mother said it was just practice so they'd all be there to cheer me on. Vance had a little hissy fit at the kitchen table. I overheard Vance begging Dad to not make him go to my "stupid piano thing." My father chose to take him to practice, and they both missed hearing me play.

Now that I'm seventeen, I kind of get it. Those recitals *were* painful to sit through. But then I contemplate—isn't that part of a family's duty? To support each other? Maybe that kind of stuff only happens on television.

I take a seat and spread the book wide. A musty smell wafts up, and I wonder when this book was last opened. My recital was eight years ago, and I haven't played since. Not even once. I stare at the notes, hoping something other than the piece's title will look familiar. My hands travel by instinct or muscle memory or magic. I'm not entirely sure which—but I'm playing.

The room fills with familiar sounds. My heart flutters. The music is satisfying. Welcoming even. The familiarity of the notes feels like safety, like home, like happiness.

As my fingers press keys, Mom's smiling face fills my head, her beaming from the audience during that last performance. The way she clapped when I stopped playing, her whispering, "Good job, honey," in my ear when I took my seat. All of it.

The piece is only a handful of minutes, three maybe, so I'm finished rather quickly. My memory slams shut.

I look up to see *Marnie* clapping and beaming, and the

image jabs at my heart. More applause comes from behind, and I wince before turning around. I don't like attention all that much. A few more nurses, a female doctor, and random family members of other patients are gathered. Everyone's smiling. The doctor asks me to play something else. I tell her I can't. She doesn't press me.

The small crowd disperses with a few more thank-you's tossed my way. Marnie pats my back. "It feels brighter in here already, hon. Thank you for sharing your talent."

My cheeks flush with awkwardness as I put back the book. "You're welcome."

I'm unsure if I should return to my father's room. Joey and Bill haven't come out yet, so my instincts are telling me to stay put and let them have their time. I take a seat on the sofa again and stare at the wall of books. I fiddle with my phone, trying to find the perfect concerto in which to lose myself.

Someone says, "I had Mrs. Gramble too."

My gaze jumps to the piano. Jacque Beaufort sits on the bench, and she's stroking the keys, petting them like a cat. "You probably don't remember, but I saw you once at her studio. I was coming out, and you were coming in. I was in second grade. You were in first."

I'm mesmerized by her voice, the fact that she's directly addressing me. I look around the room just to make sure she's not speaking to Vance. But I shake my head. Vance never took piano lessons. Vance has always been in the same grade as her.

She *is* talking to me.

VANCE

TWO YEARS AGO

DAD CAME STUMBLING OUT OF THE WOODS RIGHT AFTER I hung up on Oscar. His zipper was down, and he had some woman wrapped around him.

"Damn, Dad. Where have you been? Where's Tom?" I asked.

Before answering me, he made out with the woman. They squeezed each other's butts and growled after the kiss ended. "You like that, Growler? We sound like you!" he said.

My best friend had seen my dad tanked before so I'm pretty sure he wasn't *that* freaked out by the show going on in front of us. More groping and moaning.

"Dad!" I shouted. "Growler's gonna get grounded if we don't get the hell out of here. His mom has already called three times. He can't hold her off any longer. Is Tom gone?"

The woman giggled. My dad giggled. I wanted to tackle both of them to the ground.

"Fine. Just give me the keys. Stay here in the parking lot for all I care," I said.

Dad shook his head and came at me, like, in anger. Since I was fully sober by then, I was able to quickly move out of his way. He stumbled into our car.

My mouth unhinged. I was shocked. He'd never tried to hit me before, not even when I was little. He seriously looked like he was going to take me down.

Dad took his time turning around, and when he did, his face was wrinkled in disgust. "You sound just like your mother! So why don't you just shut the hell up, Vance? I'm living my dream, remember? I own a bar. I did that. This is *my* life! My! Life!" He grasped the door handle so he wouldn't fall.

The woman staggered to his side. He ran his hands through her long, brown hair. "I'm living my dream, right, baby? Everyone needs to leave us the fuck alone." She cooed in his face and then licked his neck.

Taking advantage of his preoccupation, I marched over and said, "Just give me the keys, Dad. Right now." Both of their eyes were slits. They were sweaty and red-faced. They were on more than weed. *Shit.* Even though he was being a dick, I didn't want to leave him there. Who knew if this lady even had a car, and there was no way either of them was driving.

I held out my hand, and Dad smacked it down. My first reaction was to take a step back. I had no idea if he'd actually take a swing at me. But instead of anger, the two of them burst into laughter.

That was it. I'd had enough. I didn't care if Dad would be pissed or not. "Hey!" The volume of my voice snapped them out of their giggle fit. "I swear to God, Dad, if you don't put the friggin' keys in my hand right now, I'm gonna freak out!"

He dropped them into my waiting palm. Growler somehow talked them into the backseat, and I drove as fast as I could without getting a ticket. Thankfully, the two of them passed out as soon as we hit I-95. Growler's mom fell for the story that my dad had struck up a conversation with our waitress at the diner (the imaginary diner we told her we were at for the last two hours) and that he may have made a real connection. It calmed her right down.

We decided to drop the wasted lovebirds off at our house first. We didn't want to run the risk of Growler's mom coming out to the car—which she did, by the way.

As soon as she walked back inside, Growler said, "If he

were my father, I'd be really pissed off. You are allowed to be angry with him, Vance. It's not fair that he's out of control all the time."

What the hell did he know? His mother was alive and breathing and calling him every five minutes to see if he was okay. He had no idea how it felt to watch his father try to fill a hole that would never be full. I gnawed on the inside of my cheek and gripped the steering wheel. "Well, he's not your father, so…"

Growler got out of the car and walked inside.

On the ride home, I replayed Dad lurching for me. I couldn't stop thinking about the way his face had looked, or the way he'd talked to me. He'd sounded like he hated me. Losing Mom was clearly eating him up inside. His drinking was at an all-time high. And this anger was new. There was no way I'd survive him turning on me.

Who would I hang out with at home? Watch sports with? Dance around the kitchen with? Who would I talk to about lacrosse and college? Dad was all I had left.

Oscar hated sports and reggae. Pretty sure Oscar hated me.

I pulled the car into the garage and sat thinking for a while. What else was Dad on? He reeked of alcohol, so there was that. And I know he got high. He did that almost every day lately. I hoped it wasn't something bad like heroin or crack.

That lady did look kind of messy. What if she was a drug addict? And she was in my house.

Oscar sat at the kitchen table looking like a scared toddler.

"They're up in his room and…" His voice trailed off.

"And what? They're having sex? News flash, little brother, that's what guys do." I was still angry with him for being such a selfish baby on the phone. *Boo-hoo, you're scared. Join the club.* I tossed the keys onto the counter and opened the fridge. An extremely loud scream or moan stopped me in mid-grab.

"They're up in his room, and *they're loud.* They're in Mom and Dad's bed," Oscar said.

Crap, I hadn't thought about it like that. I knew Dad played around with women after Mom died. I'd watched him go for it at the bar sometimes. But this was the first time he'd brought someone to the house. In Mom's bed. I never expected him to stop living or anything, and it was perfectly normal for him to be with other women, but like this? It felt all wrong.

I stood up straight and listened. Grunts, groans, and profanity assaulted our ears. My palms went slick. There was no way I'd be able to sleep up there. My room was right across the hall, and our walls were thin.

Oscar played with the salt shaker on the table. "How could he do that with someone else where *she* slept?"

Dad was self-destructing, that's how.

"What are we going to do?" he said.

I poured myself a huge glass of chocolate milk and drank half of it down. "I don't know what you're going to do." A decent burp crawled out of my mouth. "But *I'm* sleeping in the basement."

Oscar stood up. "There are two sofas down there. I'm coming with you."

"I call the maroon one."

"Whatever, Vance."

We got settled on our sofas and eventually the only sound was our breathing. I tossed and turned. I didn't like the quiet. Hadn't liked downtime since Mom died—it was too easy to get lost in the bullshit sadness of it all. I'd rather keep moving and talking and partying. And living. Way more fun.

I could tell Oscar was asleep. His nose made this little whistle. Normally I found it to be the most annoying sound in the world, and I'd typically throw a pillow at him to make him stop. But I didn't. I lay in the dark and listened to that whistle for a very long time.

Each whistle-y exhale lowered my heart rate. It took me back to when we were little and we'd fall asleep down here. On the weekends, Mom and Dad wouldn't even try to bring us up to our rooms. They'd just leave us be. They were too busy having fun up there dancing and drinking wine.

K. M. Walton

Those memories made me ache, like, my brain hurt. Everything was so destroyed. I readjusted my position again and turned on my side. My brother slept on his back, and I watched his chest rise and fall. Maybe being with Oscar back then didn't suck that much. We used to spread out our Yu-Gi-Oh! game mat down here and duel with our cards for hours. Oscar had way better monster cards than me so he'd win a lot. Now that I think of it, I don't know why I even liked playing Yu-Gi-Oh! with him. I hate losing almost as much as I hate the quiet.

So being in the basement with Oscar and his quiet-crushing nose whistle felt safe, like when I had two parents and my world was innocent. Back then, death meant nothing to me. I didn't fear it. I didn't think about it.

Sometimes after mom died, I wondered if Death had me and Oscar and Dad trapped, like he was trying to choke the last bit of life from us.

OSCAR

JACQUE CONTINUES SOFTLY RUNNING HER FINGERS along the keys. The piano is silent. My head is screaming.

"The day I saw you is such a clear memory," she says.

What? I may explode all over this Common Room. All over the books. All over the sofas. All over that piano.

She turns and looks at me. We lock eyes. Blood rushes to my face. I want to run away, but she's talking. "I remember your mom too. She had such a pretty smile. I'm so sorry about what happened." She drops her chin.

Even if I were a normal conversationalist, I don't think I'd have a response to those kind words.

Jacque crosses her arms and continues looking at her lap. "I'm also sorry I didn't go to her funeral. It was so...selfish."

She doesn't even know me. Why is she pouring out apologies like water? I'd never have expected her to show at Mom's services. I probably would've collapsed if I'd seen her there.

"I was afraid, you know?" she says. "It would've been my first time at a wake."

I should tell her it's okay, not to stress about it, but she's talking to me with genuine sincerity. I don't want her to stop. Ever.

Her leg bounces just like it did in sculpture class. "I've wanted to apologize to you for a while, but…" She takes a big breath. "Yeah. I guess we've never talked before, so it would've been kinda strange. We're talking now though. So…I'm sorry."

I nod. "It's all right."

She uncrosses her arms and sits on her hands. "That song you played was incredible. You're really good. I hated piano. I'm too much of a daydreamer. You have to be so disciplined to play. So determined. It just wasn't my thing. My father forced me to take lessons. That day was my last time at Mrs. Gramble's studio.

"I cried the whole car ride home, then while I did my homework, all through dinner, in the bath, even when my dad tucked me in. The tears worked." She laughs. "He let me quit. I think that's why I remember that day so clearly. It was the first time my dad gave in on something he was determined to

make me do. The feeling of power I had, at nine years old…"
She drops her eyes, and her chest lifts as it fills.

I'm shell-shocked, my mouth superglued.

"You know what I love though?" She looks up and waits
for my answer.

Damnit. Heart speeding. Mouth still not working. I shake
my head.

She swallows and scrunches up her nose. "You'll probably
think this is so random and that I'm a weirdo, but…" Her
voice trails off, and she swings her gaze.

If anyone in this room is a weirdo, it is *not* Jacque Beaufort.

She says, "I love when someone doesn't care what other
people think and they just are who they are."

Why is she telling me this? Is she describing what she thinks
of my brother? Is she going to ask me to put in a good word
for her with Vance?

"My mom is like that. She's got this quiet confidence,
this pride. She just believes in herself. God, I want to be like
that. She's the polar opposite of my dad. He's not a jerk or
anything. Just intense." She lowers the cover on the piano keys
and laughs. "Sorry. Wow. That was a total TMI moment."

Vance is back and standing in front of the piano. He's block-
ing my view of her. "What are you still doing here, Beaufort?"

"I was on my way out when the music filled the dead

silence," she says. Vance must make a face because she fumbles, "Oh right. Bad word choice, Irving. I shouldn't have said 'dead' silence."

"Whatever, Beaufort. Don't sweat it." He thumps the top of the piano with his fist.

I hate how a lot of the athletes at school address each other by their last names. It seems impersonal. Looking someone in the eye, saying their first name—really seeing them—is how human interaction should be done.

Does Jacque really see me?

As Vance passes—without looking at me—he says, "They're done with Dad, and they want to say goodbye. Let's go."

I get up and look toward the piano. Jacque's gone. *Of course she is.*

Vance doesn't wait for me to walk with him so I don't even try to catch up. I'm ten steps behind. When I walk into the room, he's already shaking Joey's hand. Billy wipes his cheeks with the heels of his hands.

Joey extends his hand to me, and I take it. "We're real sorry, Oscar. You know that me and Bill will do anything for you guys. All you have to do is ask. He loved you guys. I know he did. He really did." He turns to Bill. "Right, Bill?"

Bill stops patting Vance's back and nods. "You two were the best part about him, and he knew it."

He loved me? I was the best part about him? These statements are surprising to hear. Are they true?

Joey gives my hand one more squeeze and then lets me go. "On the days when you guys weren't working, he'd tell customers about his boys, that he liked how different the two of you were. Such strong personalities. You, Vance, with your ball-busting and your lacrosse, and you, Oscar, with your music and art stuff. You both made him proud. I know it. Got to where everyone felt like they were a part of your lives."

"We're family at the Blue Mountain," Bill says.

I don't want the Blue Mountain family. I want impossible things. My parents to be happily married again and alive and—

My thoughts stop abruptly as piercing new questions form. Why would my father only talk about us when we weren't there? Why couldn't he tell us we were "the best part about him" to our faces? Why are we hearing this from Joey and Bill, the bartenders?

I look at my father's mouth, wide open in a silent scream. *Talk, Dad. Please. Tell me everything.* Were *you ever proud of me?* My father discussed my art? What did he say?

I'll never be able to ask him these questions. That reality is incredibly jagged. The cut will never be clean; it will never heal properly.

There will always be a scar.

I want to scream.

VANCE

ONE YEAR AGO

Even though Dad's drinking was still intense, we hadn't had a blowout since the night of the concert. But he never did apologize for the hell he put me, Growler, and Oscar through last summer. He had just woken up and started making this huge breakfast, acting like everything was normal. That woman he'd brought home failed to resurface. Thank God. Instead of confronting him about his aggressiveness, I let it go. He probably wouldn't have remembered anyway.

However, I remember Oscar being pretty pissed off at Dad after that, not talking to him and stuff, but they never had it out or anything. Like everything else, it just faded away after some time passed.

"Let's go, Dad," I shouted upstairs. We were visiting Rutgers University today, and if we didn't get in the car, we'd miss their lacrosse team's practice, which was the whole point of the visit.

He took his time walking down the steps. "I'm moving slow today, Vance." He rubbed his forehead. I knew that translated to: I'm wickedly hungover.

Oscar and I locked eyes, and he shook his head. This had turned into Dad's daily routine. We didn't have time for what came next—coffee, sitting and staring out the window, popping ibuprofen, asking us not to talk so loud. "We can stop for coffee on the way." I grabbed the bottle of ibuprofen and shook it. "You can take these in the car."

Dad fumbled in his wallet and laid a twenty on the counter. He told Oscar to order up a pizza for lunch.

After he was caffeinated and ibuprofened, and since I knew he wanted silence, once we hit the highway I put in my earbuds and jammed to Yellowman for the rest of the drive. We arrived just as the team ran onto the field. Dad definitely rallied because he was cool when we talked to the coach and a few players. I was really impressed. The team looked solid, like, way better than WCHS. One guy pulled me aside and said I'd be a fool not to apply if I was that good.

Dad and I eventually snuck out of the academic part of the tour. We were both starving so we drove into New Brunswick and found an Irish pub. By the time we left, Dad was on a first-name basis with half the bar and I had to drive us home.

As I crossed the bridge back into Pennsylvania, he asked, "Any idea what Oscar wantsto dowithhislife?" His words ran together into a blob.

My whole face scrunched up. I clarified, "What Oscar wants to do with his life?"

He nodded. "Yesssss."

"How would I know that?"

"You're his *brother*, y-you s-smart-ass. That's how. I'm not asking the m-mailman," he slurred.

Was he that drunk? Did my father temporarily lose touch with reality? Did he not live in the same house as the two of us? Did I look like I'd suddenly started having meaningful conversations with Oscar? And why didn't *he* know? He was Oscar's father. "Yeah, well, I don't know. He probably wants to listen to violin music and draw all day. Is there a job for *that*?" I snorted.

"Nothing wrong with art."

I stared at him like he was from Mars.

"Music. Yeahhhh. Music is art. Isn't it?" He coughed and

put his head back. "Reggae reminds me of your mom. She loved dancing to it, to all of it."

I kept my eyes on the road. I used to think guys were incapable of staying faithful, that we were wired to cheat. Not that I'd had a really serious relationship, but after Mom died, I decided that way of thinking was pretty much bullshit. Cheating was a choice. Why couldn't Dad have loved Mom the way she deserved? Why did he have to rip her heart out all the time?

Dad turned to me. "Wha 'bout you?"

Wow. He sounded like his martinis had really caught up to him. I shrugged. "Does it matter?"

Dad blinked slowly. "Yesss! It matterrrrs!"

I was glad I could continue keeping my eyes on the road. "Okay. I hear you. But I wanna see how far I can go with lacrosse. Maybe go pro."

He smacked my shoulder. "You stupid? Those guys have other jobs."

I'd heard they didn't make millions, but I've always assumed they made enough to live on. *Great.* Now I needed a new plan. I went for a different tactic, one I thought Dad would like. "Why couldn't I work at the Blue Mountain?" I liked the lounge. The people. The music. The free drinks.

"The fuck you will! You're not waisssin' over a hunder grand worth of education just so you can pour b-beer for drunks!" He punched the dash and ran his hand through his hair. He was fired up.

I didn't want him flipping out on me again like before, especially not while I was driving sixty miles an hour on I-95. "Dad, chill out. Isn't the Blue Mountain your pride and joy? You always tell me you're living your dream. Why are you losing your mind? I've got over a year to figure it out. And Growler's older brother went into college not knowing. He didn't decide on a major until this year. I'm sure lots of kids have no idea what they want to focus on when they go away."

"You need to take this sssseriousssly and stop fucking around!" he yelled.

The way Dad felt about me and Oscar going to college wasn't a secret in our house. He told us all the time. He wanted the college experience and degrees for both of us. I knew it was important to him—that it was something he wished he'd done—but we were driving home from a *college visit*. How was that considered "fucking around?"

He cranked the radio, and we didn't say another word for the rest of the drive.

OSCAR

Joey and Bill say goodbye, their eyes glassy. I still think we should call Aunt Renee. I grab Dad's phone off the nightstand. "What about names of beer?" I say.

Vance looks up. "The hell you talking about now?"

"His password. Did you try beer names?" I type in "budw" and "guin" and "mill." Denied. "I just tried Budweiser, Guinness, and Miller."

"Try Red Stripe."

Red Stripe is Jamaica's national brew. "Good one." I click "reds" and shake my head.

"We're never going to figure it out. Forget it." He sounds so tired.

I can't argue with him because I agree. We will have to

wait until Dad's gone. My hand shakes as I put the cell back down.

"Tonight's gonna suck. I can't keep my eyes open. How will I count his breaths?" Vance says.

I should be thinking, *Good. Serves you right, jerk.* Instead, I see so much of my mother in Vance that it often feels like I'm looking into her eyes. Right now, his are red and worn out. "I'll do it. You can sleep." There's an unrecognizable flicker on his face. Is it gratitude?

Without looking at me, he mutters, "Thanks," and shuffles to the sofa bed I made up.

It was gratitude.

Vance is snoring in under five minutes.

There's a humming going on beneath my skin, making me energized. I could probably run around and around WCHS's track across the street.

Jacque Beaufort spoke to me.

That phrase has been auto-repeating in my brain ever since she disappeared from behind the piano.

How could I not remember seeing her at Mrs. Gramble's? I thought the first time I'd ever laid eyes on her was when she walked into sculpture. She definitely didn't go to my elementary school—I'd remember that. But our paths have crossed before I knew she existed. That's mildly exhilarating.

And *she* remembered *me*.

Dad releases another long and weary moan. Thoughts of Jacque Beaufort pop like a bubble. I spring from the chair. His head rolls off the pillow, and my heart pounds. Before readjusting him, I blow into my cupped hands to warm them up. His skin is cool to the touch. *Oh my God. Did he just die right in front of me?* I hover my hand over his mouth and feel his warm breath.

Is that relief I feel? Or disappointment? My insides are twisted.

With a careful touch I reposition his head. He sighs again. "It's me, Dad. Do you know I'm here?" My face crumples and I blink back tears. How can this shell of a man be my father? He looks like he's seventy years old. Another strenuous breath rattles from his mouth, more raspy this time. This is the most noise he's made since we got here. Maybe something's wrong.

I jog to the nurse's station and tell Marnie. On the walk down the hall, she thanks me again for playing the piano. My head bounces and I mumble, "Sure, you're welcome." Just before we're at the door, I tell her that Vance is sleeping.

She shushes herself with her pointer finger and nods.

We enter the room like ninjas and flank Dad's bed. Marnie lays the back of her hand on his cheek and then lifts the sheet from his legs. With a flick of her head, she motions for me to follow her back into the hall. She takes a huge breath before speaking. I know what she's about to say will be bad.

"It feels like his temp has dropped, and his feet looked a little swollen, honey."

My stomach has sunk to my feet.

"Do you want to sit down?" she asks. "You just went pale as a marshmallow." Marnie takes my arm and leads me to the Common Room. I drop my head into my hands as soon as I sit.

"Should I go wake your brother?"

My head snaps up. "Is Dad about to die, like, right now?"

"He could. Death doesn't follow the rules, but I think he's got some time. Maybe till morning?"

I drop my gaze and stare at the piano. "Then let Vance sleep. He needs it."

"You know those sighs he was releasing when you were talking to him? Well, some unconscious patients make those noises when a loved one is close. It's like their subconscious knows that someone they love is standing near them. So, your dad may have been letting you know that *he* knows you're here with him."

A rush of emotion floods me, and I can't stop the sob that escapes. I cover my face to hide the guilt. How can I want him to die? What the hell is wrong with me? Did I really do everything I could to help him heal from Mom's death, or did

I allow him to self-destruct? I admit that I went deeper into my shell after we lost her. It felt like my only option.

My opportunities to work on our relationship are over. They will die with my father.

I will be completely alone in this world.

The sofa dips as Marnie sits next to me. "You gotta let this out. It's not good to keep grief locked away."

Without removing my hands, I choke out my guilt and fear. I could sit here and cry all night, but I have to pull myself together. No one is with Dad right now. Not that all our needs haven't been thought of here, but the one need a hospice is *really* good at fulfilling is tissues. They're everywhere. I reach forward and grab a wad. I'm a mess.

Marnie squeezes my shoulder and leaves me be.

Even though I say I like being by myself, the thought of living as an orphan inflates an enormous balloon of terror in my chest. I stand so I can catch my breath, deflate the balloon. I walk toward Dad's room. Vance will head off to college soon and never look back. There's no doubt about that. He is annoyed by my very being.

Where will I go?

Maybe Growler's family will let me stay with them. It would only be for a year. At least until I graduate.

Then *I'll* go to college and never look back.

VANCE

IN THE NEXT FEW MONTHS AFTER RUTGERS, DAD AND I visited Villanova, Saint Joe's, and Drexel. I had to drive us home from all three.

Whatever. Dad drank martinis. At least he was interested in my future.

After meeting the four teams, talking to the coaches, and touring the campuses, I made Drexel my first choice. I could really picture myself there. It felt right. I could tell Dad was so proud when he'd tell people it was my top choice. That school had its shit together. The tour they ran was unbelievable, and they even gave us these cards with enough money loaded on them for Dad and me to get lunch at one of the restaurants around campus.

My guidance counselor and lacrosse coach were convinced I'd be getting a lacrosse scholarship of some kind, which was good, because including room and board, Drexel was over sixty grand a year. I didn't want Dad to worry about money. I mean, I knew Oscar and I had college funds, but still. Money was money, and the loss of Mom's salary took a chunk out of our lifestyle. Obviously though, the loss of Mom took a chunk out of our lives.

When I was home alone, I'd do something I was ashamed of, something I'd probably go to *my* grave with. I would stand in her closet, pull clothes out piece by piece, bring them to my face, and inhale. I just wanted to smell her.

She never wore perfume, and she wasn't into fancy beauty products. She used the same soap and shampoo that we did. But Mom smelled like Mom. It wasn't flowery or powdery or spicy. It was just her. It was home.

In the weeks after she died, the closet burst with her scent. It was overwhelming and comforting. It had been three years since then, and the last time I went in there, it took me twenty or so pulls of clothing to even catch a slight whiff.

No one knew that I'd taken one of her work blouses and put it in a plastic ziplock bag. I'd shoved it in the back of my jeans drawer and haven't touched it since. I didn't know if I'd ever open it. Her smell would be released. Gone. I couldn't handle that.

I had to be strong for Dad. I had to make him believe I was okay so he wouldn't worry about me. He had his own stuff to work through. Oscar probably thought I had bounced back too quickly. His judgment of me was kind of hard to miss. I didn't care what he thought. I cared about helping Dad get back to normal.

Oscar had his music and drawings, and no matter how stupid I thought they were, they were a place for him to retreat. To escape. Sure, I used lacrosse, but Dad had nothing. He had booze, but nothing positive. I wanted my strength to be his "something positive."

I felt like me acting like I was totally fine helped Dad, in the beginning at least. Right after she died was the worst time. He appreciated me trying to bounce back… At least I hope so. Actually, really, I have no friggin' idea, because we never talked about shit like that.

OSCAR

I swear Dad looks more yellow than when I left ten minutes ago.

"Vance. Wake up," I say.

His eyes pop open. "Is he dead?"

I toss my head back and forth. "No, but Marnie said he's shutting down."

Vance swings his legs over the side and stands. We are eye to eye. "Marnie was in here, and you didn't wake me up?" He pushes me aside and stomps to Dad's bedside. He lifts the sheet. "Does she know that his feet are swollen?"

"She does."

He glares at me, his face red. "You're an asshole, Oscar! Why didn't you wake me up?"

The fact that we continue to argue over our comatose father's body suddenly feels obscene. Dad is right here, right underneath us. My voice is barely a whisper, "I thought I'd let you sleep. You seemed wiped out. I'm sorry."

Vance attacks me every day, every single day. He enjoys upsetting me. This anger is different. He's scared. I can see it in his eyes.

"Can we not fight, please?" I say. "Not…now."

Vance gives the arm of the recliner a few fresh punches, and then we both take our seats. I take his silence as a "yes" to my question. I'm okay with this.

After some time passes, he says, "Still three breaths."

I haven't been counting. *Why haven't I been counting?* What is my problem?

"He's not going to see me graduate, is he?" Vance says.

Graduation is in five weeks. Our father probably has five *hours* to live. He will absolutely not see Vance graduate from high school. I swallow hard. He won't see me do it either. "No."

He won't meet our future wives or children. Won't cut down another Christmas tree or roast another chicken. Won't curse like a maniac when trying to parallel park. Won't dance around the Blue Mountain when his favorite reggae song comes on. I'll never hear him call me to dinner or tell Vance to play harder on the field or ask me if my homework is done.

This is it.

This is the end.

Vance says, "Do you think he knows we're here?"

"Marnie said when he sighs it could be Dad's subconscious, and that it's his way of telling us he knows we're here."

Vance winces. "I don't know if I believe that. He's in a coma."

My lips form a tight, thin line. I'm not sure I believe it either. It sounds too much like something a hospice nurse would say to a weeping son. "He's probably just breathing."

Vance turns and rests his forearms on the bed. "Dad? Can you hear me? Do you know that Oscar and I are here?"

One of Dad's regular labored breaths releases. There is no sigh.

I lean in on the bed too.

Vance keeps going. "Dad, Oscar and I are here with you. We have been the whole time. I don't know if Joey and Bill talked to you when they were here, but they came over to see you tonight."

Dad's hand jerks. Vance and I yelp.

"Holy shit! Holy shit! Why did he do that?" Vance shouts.

I panic, thinking Dad's heart stopped or something, and I repeat the same hand hovering over his mouth. When his warm breath hits my palm, I exhale along with him. "He's still alive."

"Sh-should we get Marnie?" Vance asks.

I return Dad's hand to underneath the sheet. "She was just in here. There's nothing she can do. She keeps saying he'll go when he's ready."

Vance stands and faces the window. "What if I'm not ready?"

Who is ever ready for death? Mom died suddenly. One moment she was there, and then she just wasn't. Dad's decline feels both fast and slow. We know it's coming, but we're not prepared.

"I'm not ready either," I announce sharply.

My brother doesn't turn around. He exhales onto the window, fogging it up. "Why are we arguing again?"

My eyes go wide. Typically I'm the one who acknowledges when we bicker. He's always been too busy being Vance. This is...new. "It's what we're programmed to do. We don't know how to find common ground, Vance."

He rests his forehead on the glass. "Maybe we should start trying sometime soon."

VANCE

TEN MONTHS AGO

It was the last day of junior year, and Dad was on his way to a nice buzz at two in the afternoon. Growler and I walked into the empty Blue Mountain, soaking wet. A bunch of juniors had organized a water-balloon fight out on the field. Let's just say our lacrosse skills came in handy because we nailed lots of kids with balloons. For a while, no one would throw one at me, not even my teammates. Then Growler caught me in the back, and it was on.

Dad said, "You two jackasses jump in a pool or something?" We explained and he laughed. "When are you headed to the shore, Growler?" he asked.

Growler grabbed a maraschino cherry and popped it into his mouth. "Not till August this year."

His family went to the shore every summer for two weeks. I'd been invited over the years, but my invitation was revoked after my "drinking at the prom/suspension" incident. I'd never blabbed that the hidden vodka was Growler's idea or that he was shit-faced too. He just didn't get caught. His secret was safe with me.

Maybe Dad would let me drive down for the day, and Growler's parents would change their minds and insist I stay the night. It was a long shot, but it would be worth a go when the time came.

Actually, I had no doubt Dad would give me permission. One thing my father *wasn't* was an overprotective dick. He let me and Oscar live our lives and actually do stuff. He believed that life was for living, and too much worry never did anything but make you feel like shit. That was a rock-solid philosophy.

Who wanted to sit around thinking about sad stuff? Or lock yourself away to listen to boring violin music and draw? Definitely not me. I'd rather be like Dad and *live*.

Dad put three shot glasses on the bar and filled them with Fireball. He took one and lifted it. "To the end of school, the beginning of summer, and feeling gooooood."

We each grabbed one, clinked them together, and tossed them back. "Ahhhh!"

"That burns so nice!" Growler said.

Oscar was all of a sudden standing at the end of the bar. Frowning. Sucking the fun out of the moment. *Not* living. He must've come in the back door. "You can get—"

Dad cut him off. "Shut down. Yeah, I know, you've announced that since you were thirteen. Relax, Oscar." He threw his arms out to the side. "It's all right. We're celebrating. Do you see another human being in the bar?" He laughed and held up the bottle. "You gotta live a little! Wanna join us?"

Oscar winced and shook his head.

Dad turned his back on him and cranked up the sound system. Jimmy Cliff's "Many Rivers to Cross" filled the bar, and Dad shouted, "This right here really *is* my favorite song."

My brother disappeared down the hall.

OSCAR

VANCE SITS IN THE SMALLER CHAIR, AND WE RESUME staring at Dad. His declaration of "Maybe we should start trying sometime soon" was shocking. What did he mean? Was he weighing his options with me? Would he stay after Dad died? Asking him to clarify was terrifying so I'd just dropped my eyes.

Vance refuses to go back to the pullout, but he lets me have the recliner. "What's fair is fair," he says. I swallow a laugh. He has never in his whole life subscribed to this philosophy. He's more of an "If I want it, I take it" kind of guy.

"Thanks?" I say, unsure if he'll suddenly change his mind.

I take out my sketchbook and begin a new drawing of Dad. I haven't drawn him from over here.

"What are you doing?" Vance snaps.

I lift only my gaze. "Isn't it obvious?"

"Are you seriously drawing Dad right now?"

I take a deep breath. That was a familiar tone. Here we go. "Yes, Vance, I'm seriously drawing Dad right now. Why is that a problem for you?"

He shakes his head wildly. "You're too fucking much. You really are. You make everyone around you feel like they're stupid or lower than you. You even do it to Dad sometimes. And you, you—" He stops abruptly and exhales. I remain silent. "I can't believe you have the balls to sit there with your little book and draw him. He's dying!"

What I can only describe as steam shoots from my nose. He's attacking me for drawing? We both just said we didn't want to argue! So much for trying to find common ground. If I respond, I may crack and leak and puddle. If I *don't* respond, he may lose his mind. My hands sweat. The walls suddenly crowd me. I want to run away.

Instead I clear my throat, glare at him, and find my voice. "Is this you finding common ground?"

"Stop staring at me like a psycho!" Vance's eyes just might pop from their sockets. "You're too much."

Our silent scowls duel for some time until Vance says, "Don't you have anything else to say? What's that? You're a selfish prick?"

I look down at the floor. "That's not fair."

"Fair? Do you hear yourself, Oscar? Fair? None of this is fair!" He yanks the sheet up in the air. "Dad's feet swelling like stuffed pigs, *that's* not fair! We're going to be orphans, that's not fair! You getting your feelings all bunched up because you know I'm right? Who gives a shit! Not me. It's obscene to draw him like this. It's just fucked up. Do you really think he'd want this captured in your book?" He points to our comatose father.

"Just because you've always been Dad's favorite doesn't mean you know what he wants. I can draw whatever I want. Besides, you've never laid your eyes on a single thing I've drawn." While this is true, I'm not sure it's the best response to his outburst.

Vance paces the length of the bed. "It's about you, huh? Of course it is, baby brother. Well, boo-frickin'-hoo. I've never seen the shit you've drawn. Has it ever occurred to you that you've never shared it with me? Because you haven't. Ever. Not once. But believe me, it's not like I've been too broken up about it. I seriously don't give a shit.

"You can keep your drawings. In fact, how about you shove that whole book *and* your pencils straight up your ass?" He stomps toward the door. "And let's stop pretending like you care about Dad. You want him to die! I know you do!" Vance turns away. "You're such a hypocrite." He says over his shoulder, "When Dad dies, we are completely fucked, by the way. Shit. Man, I need some air."

I'm alone with Dad. He shows no signs that he's heard the blowup between his boys, the ugly truth Vance just yelled out. Dad is just breathing. Guilt forces me to concentrate. So Vance believes everything's over for us. Maybe we should go our separate ways and live our lives. Kids lose parents every day all over the world. Who says we have to rely on each other? Where is that law?

Dad's chest rises and falls three times in a minute. I time it.

I want more time. No doubt my brother wants more time. Finally, common ground established.

"Why are you dying?" I whisper.

No response, which is not all that different from when Dad was up and around. A fresh jolt of shame shoots straight to my heart. Why is my first reaction always to go negative? Am I even capable of remembering the good?

I lean my head back and close my eyes. Dad coming home from work with new packs of Yu-Gi-Oh! cards pops into my brain. Vance and I used to lose our minds with excitement ripping those plastic packages open. Dad would stand there smiling, asking if we got any powerful monster cards. My brother and I would race to the basement to duel, and of course we'd argue. Dad did always let me and Vance duke it out on our own. It was a rarity if he stepped in. He said brothers as close in age as us had to figure it out ourselves. I think that is positive.

But after Mom died, there were times I'd stomp to my room, furious that he hadn't seized the moment to teach my brother humility, compassion, kindness. I'd usually go to bed promising myself I'd be nothing like my father if I had children.

I'm being negative again. *Damnit.* I'm hopeless.

With defiance surging through me, I resume drawing. He's my father too, and if I want to sketch him, I will. I concentrate on his face, specifically his eyes and forehead. There's no crease between his brows. It's smooth.

My father furrowed his brow whenever he talked to me. If he was interacting with me, his forehead was pinched.

Why haven't I noticed his relaxed forehead till now?

I tuck my book underneath my arm and stand to get a closer look. Flat as can be. I run my fingertips above his brow. I'm drawing him for me. Vance is right. Dad probably would be angry. But deep down, I like to think he'd understand that I *have* to draw him. I have to capture every single second he's still here. That's not selfish, is it? My hand slides down to his shoulder, and I rest it there. "Maybe it is selfish."

VANCE

EIGHT MONTHS AGO

I PARKED A BLOCK AWAY FROM GROWLER'S RENTAL house and headed to the beach. He said they were to the left of the Thirty-Fourth Street lifeguard stand. He was supposed to tell his mom I was coming to hang, like, a half hour ago, just so she wouldn't be *that* mad when she saw me.

I took off my sneakers and socks and left them at the top of the stairs. Walking on the beach with shoes on was for dorks. I spotted Growler and his mom down by the water.

"What are you doing here?" his mom said when she saw me. Not exactly in a nice way either.

"Hey, Mrs. Fulton," I said. I could tell by her pinched face that Growler hadn't softened the blow.

"Oh crap, Vance. S-sorry," he bumbled and hopped up from his chair. "Mom, I forgot to tell you that Vance was coming to hang on the beach for the day." He turned to me and mouthed, "Sorry."

I punched his shoulder and mouthed, "Fuck you."

"Hello, Vance." Growler's mother pulled her beach chair up to a sitting position and gave me a once-over. "And your father just let you drive down here by yourself? Does he even know where you are?"

Wow. Hostile. "Yes. He knows." I forced a smile, trying to pile on the charm.

"I suppose it'll be all right," she said, her lips tight. "You're only staying the day?"

"You could stay overnight, right, Vance? Didn't your dad say it was cool if you stayed over?" Growler needed to chill out. He was ruining the whole plan. Sleeping over was supposed to be *her* idea.

I watched his mom's expression. She winced. *Shit.* I was driving home tonight.

She said, "Let's play it by ear, gentlemen."

Perhaps the deal wasn't dead yet.

"We're gonna get something to eat, Mom," Growler said. He flicked his head and started walking.

"Thanks, Mrs. Fulton." She had already laid her chair back, so all I got was a wave.

As soon as we were far enough away, I said, "Dude, you almost blew it. Nice going."

"My parents got into a wicked fight this morning before my dad left. That's why she's extra salty. I forgot to ask her. But she'll cave. She always does."

We climbed the steps to the boardwalk. "You mom really hates me now, doesn't she?"

Growler stomps the sand from his feet. "She's definitely still mad about the whole drinking thing."

I had a perfect way to wipe his mom from my head. "Wanna smoke before we eat? I packed the glass bowl."

"Dumb question." Growler punches my shoulder. "My rental is right there. The house with the red roof."

"Your mom won't pop in to check on you?"

Growler shook his head. "She thinks we're eating. And she doesn't leave the beach until sundown."

We walked to his house and headed up steps to the wraparound deck, and he unlocked the door. This was a different house than they had rented the last few summers. "Whoa," I said. "This place is nice!"

"My dad got a huge bonus this year so we splurged on a house close to the beach. It's sweet, right?"

K. M. Walton

Hardwood floors, leather sofas, skylights, and a huge open kitchen. "It's sick."

"Will's not even here till tomorrow night. He's finishing up a summer course. You could sleep in his room."

Granite countertops, stainless-steel appliances, massive coffeemaker—this place was unreal. But I knew what would make this house even better. I pulled out the bowl. "Let's smoke."

"Outside. There's a gigantic shower. It's private, and the smoke'll just float away."

Growler wasn't kidding. The outside shower area was bigger than my bedroom at home, and it was tucked underneath the house. All the newer houses at the shore had to be up on wooden pilings so the houses wouldn't get slammed by the big storms. "There's even a light down here?" I said, amazed. I handed him the bowl and lighter.

He took a hit and passed it to me.

He blew the smoke straight up. "There's a bonfire on the beach tonight. Wait until you see the girls, dude. They're tan and hot."

Who knew that things would get so messed up at that bonfire? Sure as hell not me.

OSCAR

It's not until I finish smudging and shading my drawing of Dad that I realize my brother has yet to return. I fear leaving this room. What if Dad is the sort who'll wait until he's alone to die? I couldn't handle that. Vance would never recover if he wasn't here, which makes me want to go find him.

I step into the hall and I'm in luck. A nurse I haven't met yet is sitting at the rolling station. "Excuse me. Is Marnie still here?"

She looks up and smiles. "Hey, there. She's at a different post. What do you need?"

I explain that I'm afraid to leave the room, but I also need to find my brother. She offers to give the floor a look and report back.

"Thank you," I say.

Another bit of kindness from a stranger. I don't know this nurse. She's new to me. But I've yet to meet a cranky hospice employee—they're all awesome. I guess you have to be really nice to do this for a living.

She's back in no time with a dazed Vance on her arm. "He fell asleep in the Common Room." He thanks her and then shuffles to his seat. "I'm just outside if you need me." She slinks out and leaves us be. Again, more thoughtfulness.

"Look at Dad's forehead," I say, choosing to drop the argument.

Vance yawns and shrugs. "Yeah, so?"

"Really look at it."

He leans in. "I *am* reaaallly looking at it. What am I supposed to see?"

"No, look for what *isn't* there."

"I don't get it." Vance huffs.

Why is he so difficult? "The crease." I stroke Dad's forehead. "It's not there." I can tell by Vance's bewildered look that he doesn't understand. I furrow *my* brow with exaggeration. "Dad looks like that sometimes. Right here is always pinched together." I point to my forehead.

"What are you talking about?"

I huff. "Don't tell me you never noticed it before. It's always crinkled. Right here." I rub in between Dad's brows.

"Why do you care so much? I meant what I said before. I know you want him to die."

Admitting how I feel…that he's right… I can't. He would flip out again. What a mess.

Vance's cheeks redden. "You've never appreciated him! You disappeared into your cave after Mom died. You never even tried to help him…or me. And believe me, I'm not expecting you to somehow get close to Dad on his deathbed. Whatever, Oscar! You'll have to live with all that bullshit, not me." He turns his back to let me know he's done, slams down into the chair, and gets lost in his phone.

His words are like a punch in the gut. What he just said is true. All of it. My stomach grinds with this sudden reality. I should've tried harder to be present, to be there for both of them, and guess I stink at hiding how I feel. And all along I'd thought I was so good at burying my emotions behind blank stares.

I gaze at Dad's smooth forehead and count his breaths. *Now that you're about to leave me, Dad, I really don't want you to die.* "I wish he had more t-time." My voice cracks. Vance looks up so fast that I don't have time to swipe the tear running down my cheek. He glares at me. And glares. I turn away. The pain in his eyes is so intense, so sharp.

He hates me.

K. M. Walton

How will we survive this? The future? Anything?

If Vance chooses to move on without me, I will have no blood relative in my life. No one to share a family memory with. No one to commiserate this loss with. Why am I suddenly wanting things that I could've had my whole life? Maybe watching my father die a slow death has made me lose touch with reality.

An ache forms at the base of my skull. I want to crawl into a bed and sleep for days. Vance and I don't speak for a while, maybe an hour, and I'm okay with this. If Vance had kept it up, I might've blabbed my feelings out. I don't think I'm ready to admit any of that stuff to him.

Vance winces as he stands. "The sofa out in that Common Room sucks. I hurt my bad knee getting up."

I hadn't noticed him limping when he came in so I hope this is his way of letting me know that he's moved on. "Well, we're in a hospital," I say. "I'm sure they'd be able to spare two ibuprofen."

He must still be angry with me because he acts as if I've said nothing. To show him that *I've* moved on, I say, "I'll go get you some. Stay off your knee." Out of habit I take my sketchbook with me.

He doesn't look up as I pass, but he says, "Thank you."

VANCE

GROWLER'S MOM NEVER DID EXTEND THE INVITATION for me to stay the night, so I fake-left and just walked the boards until Growler could meet me.

"If the cops come, run. They've only showed up once before, and we all got away," Growler said.

"How many people come to these parties?"

"Could be twenty, could be fifty. Depends on who's down and who brought friends." He tossed his arm around my shoulder. "We're hooking up tonight, friend. No doubt. These girls love lax players down here."

We passed the last row of beachfront condos and then the

final light pole. The boardwalk ended, and we stopped to survey the dark beach. Growler pointed to a light about two football fields away. "There they are. See the fire?"

We wandered up, grabbed two beers from the keg, and started socializing. About twenty minutes and three beers later, I felt a tap on my shoulder. I turned around, and there was the hot girl from the Mann, smiling. "Hey, Vance, right?"

She remembered my name? My head bobbed, and to be cool, I took a sip from my cup.

She tilted her head, and the firelight caught her face. *Wow, still beautiful.* "So, Vance, who are you here with?"

I chugged the rest of my beer before answering her. "Well, Chrissy-with-the-boyfriend, shouldn't I be asking you that question?"

"It's Christina actually." Her mouth curled into a grin. "And you can ask me whatever you want. I don't have to answer you, but you can ask me."

Before I had time to organize a normal response, I blurted out, "Here's a question. Are you flirting with me?" *What the hell? What a dick.* I needed another beer.

She looked me in the eye. "Maybe."

"Where's your boyfriend?"

"Not here."

I smiled. "Well, that's good news."

"Wanna go for a walk?"

"Only if you promise not to take advantage of me," I said.

"I don't like to promise things unless I can fully commit."

I nodded. "So you plan on taking advantage of me out there?"

"Maybe."

I held out my hand and offered to fill our cups before we walked. Growler sat by the fire with a curly-haired girl, and they were laughing their asses off. I bent down and told him I was going for a walk. We gave each other knuckles.

Christina was waiting right where I left her. She took her full cup from me and looped her arm in mine. "So you go to West Chester High School with Jacque, right? Do you like it? Jacque never shuts up about how much she loves that school and softball, and who the hell cares, right? High school sucks. It's designed to suck. Who thought putting a thousand teenagers in varying stages of puberty together in small rooms with cranky middle-aged adults was a good idea? It's madness.

"Why couldn't school-school just end after eighth grade graduation? Then we would all have to go to cyber high school. And we wouldn't have to be perfect, or care about what to wear or who saw us trip up the stairs. We could graduate and go right to college. Everyone says college is way better and all the high school bullshit disappears. Why does high school have to exist at all? Right?"

Christina stopped dead in her tracks, and since we were linked, I stopped too. My beer sloshed out of my cup. She took a deep breath and said, "Sorry. Whoo. Wow. Vent much? I guess I'm ready for high school to be over. Can you tell?"

I liked WCHS. But to make her feel better, I told her I agreed.

A tall, white lifeguard stand loomed up ahead. We headed toward it and climbed up. We sat shoulder to shoulder. The moon was bright, and stars dotted the sky. She took a sip and then asked, "So what do you love?"

I snorted and raised my cup.

"Besides a buzz."

The waves crashed as I tried to come up with a decent answer. "Having fun."

"That's in the same category as having a buzz. What else?"

I nudged her with my shoulder. "Why do you care?"

"I don't know. It's just a question."

I echoed what she'd said earlier. "You can ask me whatever you want. I don't have to answer, but you can ask me."

She held up her cup and we toasted. "Touché, my friend."

After a minute or so I said, "Lacrosse. I love lacrosse. There."

"Why?"

"You should either be a lawyer or a shrink."

"Ew. No." She shivered. "I'm going to be an author."

I squinted and studied her face. "I could see that."

"Okay. Back to you. What's so great about lacrosse? Sports are a mystery to me. What can you possibly get from running and sweating and tossing around a little white ball?"

"I could ask you the same about books. Reading is a mystery to me."

Christina covered her ears. "I'm going to pretend you didn't just say that." She threw her head back and laughed. "Totally kidding. So, lacrosse?"

"It makes me happy."

She swung her feet back and forth. "Care to elaborate?"

"Nope."

"Fair enough."

We sat in the moonlight, Christina's head on my shoulder, and just breathed. I didn't try to kiss her, and she didn't kiss me. We hung out in the quiet until she fell asleep. In my mind, I went over all the ways lacrosse made me happy. The challenge of training, how I came alive on the field, the way my teammates and coaches respected me, even just being outside breathing in fresh air. Lacrosse was a part of me.

Christina caught herself as her head slipped off me. "Shit. Sorry, Vance. Wanna head back?"

I hopped off and helped her down. All of a sudden, she wrapped herself around me and squeezed me tight. "Thank you," she said into my neck. "This was nice, just hanging out together. You're a good guy."

Blood rushed to my crotch. *Great.* Poking her with a boner would definitely make her change her mind about me. I broke the embrace. "It *was* nice. You're nice." *What a dick.*

"Let's walk back. My friends probably think I left." She linked her arm in mine again.

I probably should've kissed her. I wanted to.

When we emerged from the darkness, all hell broke loose. Just like that.

While Christina and I were chumming it up like two old pals, her boyfriend had shown up to surprise her, and he had five buddies with him.

I had Growler.

I'll admit that it didn't look good, Christina and me coming back from a walk. Her boyfriend definitely didn't like it. No amount of "Dude, we didn't do anything" worked on him. He was wasted and full of jealous rage. Not a great combo. He came at me, and then it was a giant all-pile-on-Vance party. Growler tried to help, but he was only one guy. The two of us didn't go down easy, but yeah, we went down.

In addition to the six dudes kicking my ass, the sand played a part in my demise. It was impossible to hold my ground when the ground itself wouldn't stay still. It was like fighting on a treadmill. One guy held me from behind while boyfriend-guy popped me square in the face. When I was released, my leg twisted in the most inhuman way. I heard something snap in my knee.

Someone called the cops. The party scattered like roaches when the big flashlights and loud voices came. Growler and I would've run too, but he was knocked out cold and I couldn't even stand up. I'd tried twice, but the pain from my knee made me collapse into a moaning heap.

The cops found the weed. I failed the Breathalyzer test.

Maybe I should've kissed her.

OSCAR

I WAKE WITH A SHIVER AND SIT UP. IN A SMOOTH MOTION, I push on the lever and get the recliner upright. A rattled breath leaves Dad's body. I wait for another, which comes. He is still alive.

Vance is crumpled in the uncomfortable chair. There's no way he's going to wake up refreshed.

According to my phone, it's six twenty in the morning. Maybe Vance could get a few quality hours of sleep if I woke him and got him over on the pullout. I stare longingly at its untouched comfort. It calls to me. But I was the last one to sleep on it. What's fair *is* fair.

I give his shoulder a shake. "Vance?"

Normally my brother required multiple attempts at being

woken up, often to the point where Dad resorted to blaring music in his room. Not since we've been close to losing our father though. He's been springing awake. Like now.

"Is he dead?" he blurts out.

"Still alive."

He puffs his cheeks up with air and rubs his eyes. "Why'd you wake me then?" There's no anger in his tone, which is startling to me. His question is simply a question.

I point to the luxurious-looking pullout. "You'd probably get higher-quality sleep over there. It was your turn last night."

Vance stretches and groans. "Did you sleep?"

"Some. He's still at three breaths."

He stands and lifts the sheet, and we stare at our father's legs. Now his calves have swelled and his feet seem even puffier. We lock eyes.

Vance's eyes are screaming. My eyes are screaming.

We are together silently screaming.

Vance lets go, covering Dad's bloated limbs. "Why is Dad such a fucking mess?"

I immediately launch into the reason for his swollen legs, and Vance cuts me off. "No!" he shouts. "Not now. His whole life. How did he get this way?"

Vance's question is one I've asked myself for years, but it is shocking to hear *him* wonder. I'd always presumed Vance approved of how Dad lived his life. The partying. The lacka-daisical attitude. The women. *Now* he's asking me how Dad got this way? Now?

He adds, "Do you think it's because his parents died when he was so young?"

"We don't have to turn out like him, Vance." Saying it out loud, with Dad still breathing in and out, makes my stomach swirl. I expect my brother to launch another attack, a fresh argument.

He exhales and nods, and I am stunned.

Not turning out like Dad is important to *me*. I want to set roots and connect with the people who matter to me. I don't want to overlook stuff like he did. I want to learn from my father's mistakes and be better.

Seeing. Hearing. Loving like I mean it. That's the man I want to be.

Vance heads to the pullout, crawls in with his back to me, and curls up.

The new nurse from the hallway comes in, sees Vance, and walks gingerly toward me. "Hey, there," she whispers, "how's everyone doing in here?"

She's a very tiny and compact woman with short, dark-gray hair and a warm smile. I take in a huge breath—that is a tricky question she just asked. How is everyone doing in here? My brother is so wiped out he has forgotten that he hates me. I'm delirious, working on about two hours of fitful sleep. And my dad, well, his luck is about to run out. I'm not getting into all that with this woman. I lie, "Fine."

She tucks her lips into a grin and raises her eyebrows. "You sure about that? You look exhausted."

I shrug and nod.

"Well, let me get a look at your dad." She walks over to his bedside and scans him head to toe before touching his forearm. The blanket lifts in her grasp, and her mouth tightens into a line.

"My brother and I just saw his calves. The fact that his feet are now bigger is bad, right? That's what Barbara explained yesterday." God, that feels like years ago. So does Vance and me driving behind the ambulance. Watching them roll our unconscious father into the hospice building. Meeting Barbara, getting him situated in his own room. Her explaining why they consistently lift the sheet to check the lower half of the body.

And it was only three days ago.

"I'm sure Barb or Marnie explained how the swelling is related to the kidneys," she says.

"Barb did." I glance at her name tag and nearly swallow my tongue. Her name is Peggy. That was my mother's name. My sleepless haze last night must've prevented me from noticing her name.

"You're Oscar or Vance?" she asks.

"Oscar."

She reaches across my father's exposed legs to shake my hand. "I'm Peggy."

Even hearing her say the name aloud makes my stomach clench.

"Your dad's new swelling tells me his kidneys are slowing down." Peggy takes one of my father's hands into hers. "And his blue nail beds mean that his circulation is steering clear of the edges of his body and sending the blood to the organs instead."

Why hadn't I noticed the blue tone of his nail beds? I've been staring at him for hours. *Does this mean we'll lose him today? In a few hours? Should I wake up Vance?*

"Why don't you sit down, Oscar," she says. She's by my side in a flash, guiding me into the recliner. "You're as white as this sheet." Peggy feels my forehead. "Lean back, okay? Let me put your feet up." I do as I'm told and she pulls the chair's side handle, lifting my feet. "There you go. Sit tight. I'll be right back with some orange juice."

When I first arrived here, all I wanted was for him to die. I thought *wanting* it would prepare me. Now that the information is upon me, crushing with the weight of an elephant, with the weight of a thousand elephants, the desire for him to leave is gone. I don't want it anymore. I will reject it. Cover my ears. Close my eyes.

I fake sleep. Peggy leaves a cup of OJ on the dresser at the foot of Dad's bed. She doesn't see the circus giants sitting on my chest, their trunks trumpeting in my ears, their thick, white tusks stabbing me.

VANCE

EIGHT MONTHS AGO

THE FIRST PERSON I CALLED FROM THE EMERGENCY ROOM was Oscar. Not Dad. My fingers just auto-tapped his number. There was no way I could've spoken to Dad right out of the gate. The situation was a shit show. So, like I said, the cops found the weed, I failed the Breathalyzer test, *and* I needed major reconstructive surgery on my knee. After my MRI, they said I had the "unhappy triad of the knee." The specialist they called in nodded when I asked him if this would affect lacrosse.

Shit.

Show.

I lost it, cursing and punching the bed. The doctor actually took a step back, and two nurses appeared out of nowhere. "Vance! Calm down," the one nurse kept shouting. I tossed my head back, closed my eyes, and tried to catch my breath. My thoughts were as messy as my knee—reliving the ugly parts, jumping from thing to thing. The fight, the pain, having to face my dad, the look on the doctor's face.

Once I was sure the adults were out of the room, I opened my eyes. The first thing that came to mind was: I couldn't lose lacrosse.

My whole future was linked to it. So was my happiness. Being out on the field made everything disappear—Mom's death, Dad's drinking, Oscar's miserableness. I needed lacrosse. Really, Dad's happiness was also linked to it. The only time he smiled lately was when he watched me play.

The doctor let me have my fit, and then he clarified, "Not forever. But you've torn your anterior cruciate ligament, medial collateral ligament, *and* your medial meniscus. Your injury is severe. I'd count next season out. Lacrosse is a spring sport, right?"

With my jaw clenched and air shooting from my nostrils, I nodded.

"You'll still be in rehab next spring. Are your parents on the way?"

I gave him a blank stare and bobbed my head again. When he left, I immediately called Oscar.

After sharing the disaster I was in, it became a breathe-off on the phone between me and Oscar. He broke the silence first. "The police are going to ask for some sort of identification, Vance."

This was the technicality I couldn't figure out. "What about Joey or Bill? Couldn't they pretend to be Dad?"

"I'm certain the authorities will require some form of valid identification."

He was right. "I can't tell him, Oscar. I just can't." Deep down, I knew this was the real reason I'd called my brother. Yes, Dad was normally pretty laid-back, and he'd taken my vodka suspension in stride, but this was uncharted territory. I'd never been arrested before.

I wanted Oscar to be the one to tell our father how badly I'd fucked up. How I'd just destroyed his one positive escape.

Now all Dad had was vodka.

Oscar absorbing my dad's potential anger—shooting the messenger, kind of—could help ease the blow for me. Maybe hearing that I needed surgery and months of rehab would trigger Dad's sympathy. He'd be so worried about me that there'd be no way he'd get that pissed.

"Despite your selfish motivation for me dropping the bomb, Vance, I will tell Dad. But you owe me."

Awesome. Easier for me. He didn't say no! There was no way he was doing this out of the kindness of his heart. "What do you want?"

Oscar didn't answer for a few seconds. "I'm not sure yet."

"Fine." Whatever he wanted I could handle. "Why are you doing this for me?"

"I honestly don't know."

Dad went to the police station first, paid the underage drinking fine of five hundred fifty dollars, found out my court date for the weed possession, picked me up from the ER, and drove me straight to the Sports Medicine Center at Jefferson in Philly. He didn't say a single word to me. That was a first. He and I always talked. Talking with Dad was something that came easy for both of us.

His silent treatment freaked me out so much that I couldn't sleep during the long drive. Miles and miles whizzed by, and my stomach refused to chill out. I swear I almost puked when we hit the Walt Whitman Bridge.

Growler offered to drive my car home, but not for, like, a while. One of the jealous dick's friends broke his nose, so his mom wanted him to rest. His mom also said he wasn't allowed to hang out with me anymore. She said Dad was raising me to be a wild animal. She hated me that much. *I* hated when adults were all high and mighty, acting like they never made a mistake when they were younger. Teenagers were wired to fuck up. Duh.

Growler said she'd calm down after the dust settled, and he'd get her to change her mind about the no-Vance rule. How could she stop us from hanging at school? Her new rule was dumb.

The orthopedic surgeon at Jefferson saw me so fast because he knew Dad. He lived in West Chester and came into the Blue Mountain sometimes. I didn't recognize him, but he was a good guy, a real straight shooter. He said my knee was "mangled" and one of the nastiest unhappy triads he'd ever seen. He preferred I was admitted rather than going home. He said doing the surgery sooner rather than later would only help me in the long run with lacrosse. So he had it scheduled for the next morning.

Dad didn't speak to me until we were alone in the room. He shouted, "I am so angry right now I could choke you!"

My whole body jerked, including my leg. "Ahhhh, shit."

"You feel that pain! You deserve it."

Wow, so he definitely wasn't taking the sympathy route. He'd never yelled at me like that. I blew out a long breath and tried changing the direction of the conversation. "Good thing there's a week of summer vacation left, right?"

He acted like I hadn't said a word. "You will work off the seventeen hundred dollars you owe me at the bar. Let's get that clear."

"Seventeen hundred?" I yelled.

Without looking at me he said, "Five hundred and fifty dollars for the underage drinking fine, fifty dollars in gas, thousand-dollar emergency room copay from Shore Memorial Hospital, hundred-dollar specialist copay for the guy you just saw. Seventeen hundred. Do the math."

There went any dough I wanted to save for college spending money. "I'll work it off," I said boldly.

He shook his head. "You think you have all the answers, don't you, Vance? Well, guess what, son. You don't know shit."

I knew better than to respond. Not when he was *this* angry.

Dad stared out the window, but he had more to say. "I'm canceling our trip to Jamaica. You don't deserve it."

Shit. "Aw, Dad, come on." That was my graduation present. I already told everyone about it. How embarrassing.

"You think I'm going to waste thousands of dollars on you? After this bullshit you just pulled? And since I'm blowing your mind with bad news, I'll keep it going. There's no way Drexel won't find out about this. Especially the drug charges. Your scholarship will be no more. And when that happens, know this: you're on your own for tuition. I'll move your college fund over to Oscar. Maybe he'll get into Harvard or Yale or some shit. Who knows? But *you* will have to shoot much lower next time around." He rubbed his neck and blew air out. "I've gotta get back to the bar. Anything you'd like me to pick up from home and bring back tomorrow morning?"

He was just venting. He wouldn't give my college fund to Oscar. Would he? I clenched my jaw. Maybe he would. Losing Drexel would destroy me, and it would definitely kill Dad. Hearing the news of my scholarship had made him so happy. He'd made this huge spaghetti-and-meatball dinner to celebrate. The two of us jammed to reggae and danced around the kitchen, and we didn't even stop when stick-in-the-mud Oscar came in whining that it was too loud for him to do his math homework. Dad told him to do the homework later and come join us. Oscar threw his hands in the air and marched upstairs. Dad shrugged and turned it up, and we laughed until we couldn't breathe.

I couldn't rob him of that happiness.

Dad stood up and crossed his arms. "And it was real shitty of you to dump *your* disaster onto your brother's shoulders. He gave himself a wicked tension headache over having to tell me about the mess you were in. I have never been more pissed off at you than right now. How could you do this to me?"

Shit, he might never forgive me.

"Thank God your mother isn't here to watch your downward spiral. Saying you want to be a bartender, getting shit-faced on vodka at a dance, and now this crap. Jesus, Vance. What, are you trying to turn out like me?"

He was bringing up Mom? That was a low, low blow. My stomach flattened with the sudden weight of her absence.

I needed "party Dad" to show up.

The guy who clinked my shot glass at the Blue Mountain. The guy who told me life was too short to worry about "stupid shit." Why couldn't he have been there? He'd understand this mistake.

Dad's face was practically purple, and beads of sweat formed on his upper lip. He looked me square in the eye and said, "You straight-up just ruined your entire future."

OSCAR

VANCE SHAKES *ME* AWAKE THIS TIME. "DAD'S BREATHING sounds really messed up."

I wipe the drool from my cheek and sit up. I hear it right away. It's thick and choppy. Almost like he's congested. "How long has he been doing that?" I ask.

"I've been awake for over an hour, but it just started. Two minutes maybe."

We both go to lift the sheet at the same time. I pull back. Vance raises it and squints. "Oh shit, his skin looks gray."

"We need Peggy."

Vance's eyes bulge. "What did you just say?"

I'm already to the door so I answer him over my shoulder. "The nurse. We need her." He's obviously repeating my reaction to her name. No doubt Vance is missing Mom too right now.

Peggy isn't at the rolling nurse's cart so I jog down the hall. Most of the patient doors are closed, for which I'm thankful. I'm too full of my own pain to absorb anyone else's. The top of Peggy's head is visible as I approach the nurse's station. She looks up.

"My dad is breathing really weird, and his legs look awful." I'm out of breath from my sprint down the hall.

"Is it a rattling sound?"

I nod.

Peggy puts down her pen and stands. "I'll walk back with you."

Vance is holding Dad's hand when we walk in. "His fingernails are blue!" Another messy breath rattles from Dad's lungs.

Peggy stands at the foot of his bed. "If you haven't said what you need to say to your dad, boys, now is the time."

Her words sink into my skin. I'm so heavy.

She asks us if we'd like to say our goodbye alone or together. My lips are made of lead. They're too dense to move.

Vance answers her. "Alone."

I walk out and head to the Common Room. Peggy says from behind, "Oscar, don't go too far. I'd wait right here." She points to a wall just outside Dad's door. I turn on my heels and stand where she told me to.

Peggy says she'll be back. That's all she says. She doesn't say she'll be back after he dies, which is what she means. She just says she'll be back. I close my eyes and slide down the wall. I am a solid block of agony.

I honestly don't know how much time passes before my brother emerges and tells me it's my turn. Minutes, hours, days? I'm sinking into the tan carpet. When I make no move to stand, Vance reaches down and helps me up. His eyes are red, his cheeks flushed. When I'm standing, he goes to walk away. I repeat what Peggy said, and he takes my spot against the wall.

Dad's rattling breath greets me as I enter his room. I study his face, taking in every line and angle. I want to remember him clearly, even this part. The bed dips as I sit on the edge. "Dad, I want to believe that you can hear me right now. I *have* to believe it. I've been thinking about what I want to say to you, but I don't know. I'm not sure which death I hate more, Mom's when we had no warning, or yours when we had too long of a warning."

I take his hand into mine. "This is h-hard." I stumble as the tears come. Everything shakes. My stomach. My shoulders. My head. "I'm sorry I wasn't the son you wanted."

As soon as the words leave my mouth, I pause. Wait. *Am I sorry?*

I shake my head with enough zest that tears fly from my cheeks.

I am not sorry.

I can't let my last words to my father be untrue.

A wave of indignation suddenly bubbles to the surface. "No, Dad, I'm really not sorry about who I am. I wish you had accepted me. I wish you had encouraged me to be the best me possible instead of constantly trying to squeeze me into your predetermined frame."

Wait, I scream in my head. That's not how I want to end things either!

"W-what will we do, Dad? What are we going to do w-without you?" I squeeze his hand. *Stop asking him questions! Say something that matters!* I swallow air, spit, pain.

I blubber, "I'd give anything to have more time with you. I swear we could've worked stuff out. Oh God. I'm sorry I wasted the time we had. I'm sorry I wanted you to die when we first got here. But you understand why, right? I was so angry at you. I was always so mad at you."

I squeeze his hand.

"I *do* love you."

I close my eyes and conjure up Mozart's Piano Concerto

No. 27. I need beauty. Calm. I need something peaceful right now. My thumb rubs along Dad's pointer finger with each lift and sway of the music in my head.

Joey and Bill said he was proud of us. He must've liked being a father, even *my* father…sometimes. The music stops, my brain goes silent, and I study him. "Why did you have such a hard time? What were you so afraid of, Dad? Was it me? Was it getting sober?"

Just before his car accident, I remember Dad announcing at dinner that he was going to try and reel it in. He meant his drinking. Vance and I knew that. This wasn't his first announcement. But this time felt different, like, maybe he actually meant it. I'd asked if he was going to AA—because everyone knows it's almost unheard of to stop drinking without help—and in true Dad form, he freaked out on me. He accused me of not having faith in him. Vance joined in, agreeing with him, naturally, and I remember leaving the table about as defeated as ever.

In the two-against-one scenario, it sucks to be the one.

You know what else sucks? His version of reeling it in consisted of him only drinking half the bottle of vodka, not the whole thing. That scenario only lasted two nights. Then it was game on again. Cue the car accident. Cue the end.

"We really all fell apart after we lost Mom, didn't we? You

with your vodka, Vance with his knee, and me…me with…"
My voice trails off. I drop my chin. *Me?* I was never together.
Mom's death made me retreat *more*. I had always been hunched
down, unresponsive, separate.

"Oh, God, Dad. I-I—" I stutter and stop to grab a tissue.
"I don't want to be alone. I don't want to be alone."

I repeat that sentence in my head and stare at him for a
while. "I-I love you, Dad. I hope you find peace." His breathing suddenly sounds even worse so I go get Vance. We're both
past caring about crying in front of each other, which is weird
because I don't even remember him crying at Mom's funeral.
"H-he doesn't sound good, Vance."

Vance follows me back in, and we each take a chair. Neither
of us has any words left so we just stare at him. I grab one of
Dad's hands and Vance takes his other. An especially long and
labored breath leaves his body. I wait for the next.

It never comes.

VANCE

SEVEN MONTHS AGO

Dad was right about a lot of stuff.

He never *had* been angrier with me.

My entire future *was* straight-up ruined.

The shit show continued.

Senior year started with me in a wheelchair. I wasn't allowed to put any pressure on my knee. My surgery was a week before that. They had to graft some of my hamstring to reconstruct my ACL. Yeah, it was as effing painful as it sounded. My surgeon said he'd only seen two other knees as messed up as mine, and one was a Philadelphia Eagle. He said he was "fairly confident" that I'd play lacrosse again, just not at the level I was used to playing. He told me and Dad as if he were breaking the news of someone's death. I guess at a sports medicine facility that kind of news *is* like a death.

Even though Dad and I knew my scholarship was in jeopardy, we never talked about it. I didn't mind, believe me. Looking at his face and seeing disappointment would've shredded me.

When I started rehab, it hurt so bad that I cried in the bathroom. In the stall, I decided I *had* to play lacrosse for Drexel. I had to make Dad proud again. Six months was all I had left to work as hard as I could to get my life back.

My lawyer (yes, I had to get a lawyer) had my court date for the weed possession pushed back till the end of September on account of my surgery. He swore my penalty would be reasonable since it was my first offense. He thought I'd get drug counseling and a six-month probation. We'd have to wait and see.

I usually went straight home at the end of the school day, and since Growler's mom wasn't letting him hang with me yet, Oscar had to drive me. But now that rehab had started, he had to drop me off there, and it was all the way over near the mall.

"Is the front seat back as far as it will go?" I asked Oscar as I crutched my way to the car. The full-time crutch use was new. I was glad I didn't have to sit in that wheelchair anymore.

"You've asked me that every day, and the answer remains the same. Yes."

"Whatever, dude. If you had to deal with this shit all day, you'd ask too."

He huffed and mouthed, "Whatever."

I refused his offers of help into or out of the car. I did let him carry my backpack though. It was pretty tricky crutching around with it, and I almost took a spill the first day on them. Some teacher caught me just as I was about to go down. He insisted I let Oscar carry the backpack. So I did.

"I've got a considerable amount of homework tonight so I'd like to get you to rehab quickly," Oscar said. He took my crutches and laid them across the backseat.

"Don't speed. You just got your license a month ago."

He gave me a look. "I waited till I was seventeen, remember? And I'm not you."

As we pulled into a parking space, Oscar said, "You still owe me for breaking the news to Dad."

"I'm not in the mood to negotiate." I opened the door and gingerly got my legs out. Oscar was right there with my crutches.

"Who said anything about negotiation? I'm simply reminding you. I still haven't decided what I want from you."

I rolled my eyes. "I'll wait on pins and needles." With as much speed as I could muster, I crutched away.

"Dad's coming to get you," he shouted after me.

I gave an A-OK without turning around and went inside.

OSCAR

"Oh my God. Did he just die?" Vance asks.

I hover my hand over Dad's mouth. Nothing. There is nothing.

"Do you feel anything?" he asks.

"N-no," I choke. Unstoppable tears dump onto my cheeks.

Vance crumbles into the chair behind him and buries his head in his hands. His sobs are deep and choppy. He repeats, "Oh my God. Oh my God."

I don't want to release my father's hand. It feels exactly like it did a moment ago, when he was alive. How can that be? *I'm so sorry for wishing you dead, Dad!* What kind of an asshole son am I?

Dad's head has dipped down, and I don't like it. When I go

to "rearrange his melon" Vance shrieks, "What are you doing? Stop! Stop! Don't touch him!"

I'm so startled that I drop Dad's hand, and his arm flops out to the side. It's dangling over the edge. There's a knock on the door, and Jacque Beaufort walks in. Vance yells, "Not now!"

This scene has obviously freaked her out because she recoils, apologizes, and runs out.

Peggy is suddenly at Vance's side, but she takes a step back. He is in a full-on rage. His face is purple, he keeps punching the seat of the chair, and he's actually growling. She lets him carry on for a good two minutes before trying to calm him down. "Vance? Vance!" she shouts. He freezes mid-punch and lifts his eyes. "You can either try to calm yourself down, or I can call down to Thomas and he can help you calm down." Peggy turns to me. "Thomas is six-five and three hundred pounds."

Vance releases his fist and falls on his knees. He sobs into his elbow. Peggy sits in the chair and talks softly to him. I reach over and straighten my father's head. His skin is noticeably cooler. He is really, really gone. My stomach lurches. I need out of this room.

I barrel around the bed and stumble into the hall. Jacque is nowhere to be found, and for this I'm thankful.

Where can I go? Vance's car is locked. School is in full swing over there so I can't walk outside. Is there a bathroom close by? I have no destination but I move. As I'm about to pass the empty Common Room, the piano catches my eye. I pause and stare. All of a sudden, another Mozart piece plays in my mind: Requiem in D minor. I can actually hear the beginning with the violins, the choir. I pull my phone from my pocket and type the name of the piece into iTunes search. I tap the play button, and the sad notes fill the quiet room.

I drag one of the chairs over to face the window. I sit and cry and listen to Mozart. I would give anything for my music to have its normal effect on me. Calming yet thrilling. Peaceful and fulfilling.

Right now, it's simply recognizable noise.

Dad is gone. I never got to look him in the eye and get to the bottom of our layered and complicated relationship. The most important consistency in my life—having a living parent—no longer exists. Dinners at home, *having* a home, my job at the bar were constants, things that equaled family to me. Will any of them continue? How can they without Dad? He was the last bit of glue we had.

I shake my head as this realization takes shape.

Dad, my God, I can't believe you're gone.

VANCE

SIX MONTHS AGO

MY LAWYER WAS DEAD-ON ABOUT WHAT THE JUDGE would give me: probation and counseling. For probation I was ordered to attend school regularly, which I did; hold a steady part-time job once my knee healed, which I had; and meet with a probation officer, which I wasn't too excited about. Since my shit show had happened in New Jersey, my lawyer requested that I be allowed to work with a Pennsylvania probation officer and counselor. The judge agreed.

For the last two weeks of September, my schedule had been: Monday counseling, Tuesday physical therapy, Wednesday probation officer, Thursday physical therapy, Friday collapse.

Counseling consisted of me with a group of other kids my age in various degrees of addiction and disaster. Some had been expelled from school, others kicked out of their homes, one girl never said a single word, one dude cried every time. The group members changed a lot so it was hard to get invested in them or their stories. I never said too much but I listened. The therapist was an okay guy, not very inspiring, kind of just going through the motions.

At the conclusion of each session, I'd walk out thinking what a huge waste of time it all was. And not that I'm, like, really in favor of making kids go to therapy or anything, but the sessions really were a pile of missed opportunities. Some of those kids were pretty messed up emotionally, and they could've used inspiration.

It was Wednesday so I sat across from Mr. Richards, my probation officer, for our second check-in. He was a big guy with a shaved head and thick, black-rimmed glasses. The first time we met him, Dad and I said his handshake practically squeezed the life out of us. He was obviously letting us know he was all man. My pinkie ached for an hour afterward. I got the message.

"Let's get started," he said. Mr. Richards was cranky and serious, which I could handle because he didn't waste time on friendly shit. So in addition to being all man, he was also all business.

His office was small and cramped and filled with nothing but filing cabinets and Eagles paraphernalia. There were bobbleheads, player figurines, framed ticket stubs. Folded jerseys, footballs, posters. This guy was a hard-core fan.

His desk was covered in neat stacks of paper, along with a laptop and an enormous office phone. Seriously, that phone had three rows of preset buttons *and* a dial pad.

"I'd like to stick with weekly meetings till the end of the month and then go to every other week. Assuming, of course, you continue to keep your end of the bargain."

"Okay." My end of the bargain meant counseling, clean drug tests, school, and work.

He dropped his eyes and began filling out a paper from my file. "We'll reassess midpoint, which'll take us to Christmas."

"And this ends in March, right?"

Mr. Richards's hand froze, and he lifted his brows. "Let's take this one day at a time, Vance."

I nodded slowly.

He went through the same boring stuff as last week, and then we were done. I limped back toward the car. Each step hurt like hell, like a sharp, stabby pain. My physical therapist said recovery from my injury was one of the longest and that I'd have pain for a pretty long time.

Oscar had dropped me off at the front door so I wouldn't

have to walk far. Since the probation meetings were over in twenty minutes, he'd decided to just wait in the car. I scanned the lot and saw that he wasn't too far away. As I got closer, I could see that he had his homework spread out all over the front seats. I tapped on the hood and startled him.

"Damnit!" he shouted.

I grinned. Scaring the crap out of him hadn't gotten old yet.

"God, Vance! You made me rip my notebook page," he said. Oscar was so damn uptight.

By the time I got situated in the front seat, I'd lost the urge to apologize. So I let it go.

He turned onto the road. "When can you drive yourself around? I'm unequivocally over being your chauffeur."

I clutched my chest. "Aw, come on, little brother, you're breaking my heart. You mean you're not loving our extra time together?"

He stared straight ahead and acted as if I hadn't said a word. Why didn't he have a fully formed sense of humor? I swear it felt like he was part cranky old man. "I'm obviously kidding, Oscar. You're always a total buzzkill."

He huffed. "Oh right, *I'm* killing your buzz. Maybe you should stop chasing the party and learn how to be quiet."

"I haven't partied since the beach, so how about *you* be quiet?"

"Whatever, Vance. You know as well as I do that when your knee heals, you'll be back to numbing yourself up, and then you and Dad can party your feelings away."

A huge semitruck whizzed past, shooting a whoosh of air into my face. I just wanted to live. I wanted to feel alive and know that I was present and accounted for. What was wrong with having fun? Oscar wouldn't know how to lighten up even if he went to Fun School and studied fun. My brother was mind-numbingly un-fun.

"Me driving myself can't come soon enough, shithead," I said. "Believe me."

OSCAR

Since my back is to the world, I let myself fall apart. My face slick with tears, my mouth open and twisted, my sobs loud. I can't bear to be near his body. Not when it is already starting to get cold.

Did I say what I wanted to say? Was my goodbye enough? Will I ever forgive myself for wanting his death to come sooner? I have no answers. Things that will never happen again torture me: I'll never hear his voice, buy him another Father's Day gift, see him smile, drive in the car with him, watch him serve customers behind the bar.

None of it.

I wasted so many moments while he was alive by being

moody and jealous. It was so easy to resent the fun he and Vance always had. Why didn't I ever join them?

I should've joined them.

After a while I'm dry. I am unable to shed another tear. No one has bothered me since I've been in the Common Room, which is very thoughtful. It's most likely hospice protocol to let family members grieve privately. I wonder how my brother is, if he's still in there with Dad. Maybe we should be together right now. Before walking back, I use a bunch of tissues to clean up my face.

Just before I enter Dad's room, a terrifying thought jabs me: I am an orphan.

Vance will be the only person to whom I can say, "Do you remember when Dad..." If my brother pulls away from me—which is absolutely possible, considering our relationship—I will be alone.

I'm just outside Dad's room, and I can hear Vance crying. The sound catapults me back to when we got the news of Mom's death. The heartbreak, the despair, the fear—it's all there in that miserable sound. The door glides open, and the scene before me rips a fresh hole in my heart. Vance has the chair pulled up to Dad's bedside, as close as he can get it, and his head rests on the mattress. And he is bawling.

Somehow my body produces more tears, and they spill

over. I walk to the other side of the bed. Vance lifts his head. We lock eyes, desperately searching each other's gaze for something, anything. He drops his chin as his body shakes with sobs.

There aren't any useful words to say so we don't talk.

Dad looks awful, and I desperately want to close his mouth. His skin has taken on a yellowish-gray tone that looks about as far from living as possible.

After a while the room goes silent. Vance and I are cried out. It is in this quiet that I glue my eyes to my father's chest. It's still as stone. His labored breaths are done. *What are we going to do without him?*

A light knock on the open door makes us both turn and look. It's Peggy. "Just so you know, boys, you can sit with your dad as long as you like. We don't put a time limit on things here."

Vance sniffles, nods, and stands.

"When you're ready, come and get one of us, and we'll explain what happens next. Take all the time you need here with him, okay?"

I bob my head this time. She does the same before heading back into the hall.

Vance and I are alone with our father's body, again.

"D-dad was too y-young to die. He was too fucking

young!" Vance gets louder with each exclamation. "This can't be h-happening!" His eyes leak, sending fresh tears down his cheeks. He runs his hands through his hair as he paces. I think he's about to punch something. What he just said is true, except the "this can't be happening part." It has already happened. We are currently in what Vance would call a "shit storm."

My mother would be hugging us, kissing our foreheads and telling us we'd be okay, but she's been gone for three years now. I haven't had a hug since her funeral.

I wish I had the guts to go embrace my brother, squeeze him tight, so we could share this heavy sadness. But I don't want to get punched in the face. He looks like he's about to blow.

Vance continues going from bed to sitting room and back. "How can he be dead? We have no parents, Oscar! What are we going to do without Dad?"

I clear my throat. "That's what I keep asking myself. What are we going to do without him?"

He kicks the side of the dresser. The lamp wobbles, and my arm shoots out to steady it. I don't want Vance to get in trouble for losing it again.

"Maybe we should tell them we're done. Are we done?" I ask.

　　　　　　　　　　　　　　　　　K. M. Walton

Vance turns back to the bed. "The thought of him lying in some freezer all alone makes me want to puke."

I hadn't thought of that, and I shiver. The image of him on a metal gurney, all alone in the morgue produces a wave of nausea. I actually *may* vomit. I throw my head back and take in a huge breath through my nose. The queasy feeling remains.

We need someone to come and tell us we're done. We have no idea what we're doing. Why won't they help us? We're drowning in here. Tiny white stars flicker in my eyes. I can't catch my breath. My whole body is on fire. I stumble backward and—

VANCE

YOU KNOW THOSE SCARED-STRAIGHT SHOWS? THE ONES where the army guy or ex-cop went all hardcore on badass kids and tried to reform them?

I didn't need that.

I was completely hell-bent on getting my knee strong so I wouldn't lose my Drexel scholarship. By some miracle, Drexel remained in the dark about my arrest and my injury, so I still had my early commitment and full scholarship. Everyone in my counseling group said that since my arrest wasn't big time and all over the news, Drexel probably would never find out. My dad was psyched about that bit of information. He said it was the only good thing he'd heard about me lately. Even though that stung a little, he was right, so I didn't argue.

But my injury was what kept me up at night. Both the ER doctor and my surgeon had said I'd probably never play at the level I was used to. I chose not to believe them. Instead I gritted my teeth, sucked up the pain, and worked harder than anyone in my rehab. It didn't matter which physical therapist I had working me out—I blew their mind every single time.

That was keeping me clean. My drug counselor must've told me how proud I should be of myself, like, a million times. What I'd said to Oscar was true. I hadn't partied since the bonfire. In the beginning, my lack of energy helped me turn down the invitations, but after a while kids stopped asking, so I wasn't patting myself on the back too hard. This injury officially kicked my ass. It also kicked my social life's ass.

My schedule didn't help matters either. I usually went straight from whatever thing I had after school to the bar to work.

Today was one of those rare Thursdays when my physical therapy got canceled at the last minute. I told Oscar to just go; I wanted to walk to the bar. The day was clear and crisp so I sat on the sidelines watching the football team run drills. Since I couldn't play a sport, I got a rush watching other people do their stuff on the field. I even started going to WCHS's ice hockey games.

Growler walked up and sat next to me. "You *do* know football has the most knee injuries, right?"

I tightened my brow. "No, it doesn't. Basketball does," I said with absolute authority. Let's just say I'd become an expert on sports injuries, especially knee-related.

His mouth slid to the side. "Hmm. Maybe you're right."

"I *am* right. Hello." I pointed to my knee. "It's all I've talked about four days a week for the past three months."

We watched the players run routes for a little while. The sun went behind a block of clouds, making the already cool November day go friggin' cold.

Growler pointed to the field. "Liam's having a party tomorrow night. Wanna go?"

"I'm working," I lied. It was my go-to excuse when Growler asked me to party.

"Damn. Your dad's a slave driver." He snorted. "It's after their play-off game, which they're going to win. Look at them out there!" He cupped his mouth and shouted, "They're animals!"

I didn't want to be around alcohol or weed. I wasn't ready yet. Couldn't tell Growler that, but it was the truth.

"Everyone's going. Come on, Vance. People'll be psyched to see you out."

"Can't go, dude. Drop it." I stood up and changed the subject. "Let's go get coffee."

K. M. Walton

"The Black Bean?" Growler asked.

The Black Bean was the coffee shop in town. "I feel like walking. It'll be good to loosen me up."

Growler nodded, and we crossed the end zone.

"When did they say you'd stop limping?" he asked.

I shoved my hands deep into my hoodie pockets. "They didn't." Growler's real question was: When did they say you could play lacrosse? Even though practice wouldn't start till spring, it was usually one of our main topics of conversation. Growler hardly brought it up anymore.

I'd made the decision that I'd see how I felt once practice started up. But four months of rehab remained, so I had time on my side. Time and determination.

No way I was going to let my scholarship go. I had to fight and claw my way back to a full recovery. For me, yes, but also for my dad. Things needed to be like they were before. Dad eventually came around and stopped just barking orders at me, but it felt different. He would watch me out of the corner of his eye and pretend not to. He had stopped dancing, stopped smiling, and drank himself into a slurring, unhappy mess every night.

His pride in me needed to come alive. I had to bring his happiness back.

"You guys going to Sugarloaf again for Thanksgiving?"

I hadn't thought about that. Last year, Dad had talked about it every night once Halloween hit. This year, he hadn't mentioned a word. We went skiing up there the Thanksgiving after Mom died. Dad said it would do us all good to get away from the house, and he was so right. Skiing at Sugarloaf meant we didn't have to be in our silent kitchen. Mom always cooked a big feast for us.

I couldn't ski. Shit, I was still gimping around. "Probably not," I said. My physical therapists would lose their minds if I tried to ski.

Growler scrunched up his face. "Stupid question. Sorry, dude."

I changed the subject. "You going to your aunt's in Reading?"

"As usual."

We walked a block without talking. That wasn't an unusual thing for us to do, but now it felt awkward, like we were both thinking things we couldn't say. My mind was locked on the fact that we'd be home for Thanksgiving—home without Mom.

Growler grabbed my arm and yanked me back. "Whoa!"

A car whizzed by. My eyes went wide.

"You seriously were going to walk across, weren't you? I just saved your life. High-five." His hand hovered in the air.

I folded in half and leaned on my knees. What was my problem?

OSCAR

I come to in the recliner. Vance and Peggy stand at my feet, talking to each other. They don't know I'm conscious. I listen.

Vance says, "I can't believe he just passed out like that. Is he going to be all right?"

A lump forms in the back of my throat. My brother is worried about me—maybe for the first time in his life.

Peggy says, "He'll be okay. His vital signs are good. Let's let him wake up on his own." The room goes quiet for a few minutes, and then she adds, "The social worker is on her way. She'll do everything she can so that you and Oscar make it through this."

"Is it the same lady we met at the hospital?" Vance asks.

"Most likely."

They turn and look at the bed. I snap my eyes closed.

Vance exhales. "Where will my dad go from here?"

"The funeral home. You give me the word, and I'll start everything in motion."

"I'm going to get Oscar up. He can't be passed out when they take our dad away." I'm being shaken. "Hey, they're coming for Dad soon."

Vance has just considered my feelings. Another first. Tears well in my eyes and spill onto my face. I'm not worried about these waterworks. Vance will assume they're for Dad.

I sit up and nod.

Peggy bends down. "How you doing, Oscar?" When I go to stand, she holds up her hands. "Whoa, whoa. Not so fast, hon. We don't want you passing out again. Just sit there for a few minutes. Let's do this in stages. All right?"

She hands me a box of tissues, and even though I feel fine, I comply with her request.

"How much time do we have left with him?" I ask.

Peggy repeats her earlier statement that it's up to us when she sets things in motion. My brother and I look at Dad. Neither of us wants to be the catalyst for whatever "things" come next. She clears her throat. "How about I leave you guys alone? Just come get me when you're ready." She closes the door on her way out.

　　　　　　　　　　　　　　　　K. M. Walton

I notice that someone has lowered Dad's bed because his upper body is no longer slightly elevated. He's lying flat now, which is good because his head and neck look comfortable.

"What are we going to do without him, Oscar?" Vance's voice cracks and he looks away.

This is certainly the million-dollar question as of late. "I don't know."

Vance stares out the window, and I can't take my eyes off Dad. After a while, we switch places and more time passes. Eventually we're both sitting and looking at our father, crying openly, passing the tissue box back and forth over his body.

Vance blows his nose. "You know what I can't stop thinking about? The three of us going to Jamaica. I really thought being there would turn him around. Like, maybe all of us being together like that, relaxing, having fun, would've made him have an aha moment. A moment where he could've seen things clearly. See that he wanted to get back on track. I was so ready for him to start being Dad again."

My heart aches hearing my brother open up like this. I've longed for it my entire life, yet it's so foreign to me. I don't want to respond incorrectly and shut him down, so I nod. Vance returns the gesture. A whirlwind explodes in my gut. We just had an emotional exchange, and it wasn't based on anger.

And I know exactly what he meant when he said he was

ready for Dad to start being Dad again. Even though we never discussed it, Vance and I watched him unravel after we lost Mom—the drinking, the vomiting, the hangovers, the anger, the rage, the excuses. In many ways my brother and I became *his* parent. Teenagers aren't supposed to clean up their father's vomit or make sure the cabinet always had ibuprofen. They just aren't.

A new surge of sadness wells. Dad will never get the chance to heal. He died broken.

After a while Vance says, "I don't want to get Peggy yet, do you?"

Truthfully, I don't, but then I think that we're avoiding the inevitable. "How long has it been since he passed?"

"Why? Do you think we should get her?" Vance pulls out his phone. "It's been, like, an hour and a half."

"No, I don't, but I wish it wasn't a decision we had to make."

We sit and cry and pass the tissues over and over until the box is empty, and it is the single most brotherly experience I've had to date with him.

Vance puts the box on the nightstand. "Let's go get Peggy."

VANCE

FOUR MONTHS AGO

"Whoooo! This'll burn so good," Dad exclaimed. He held up his official eggnog mug for a toast. I lifted mine. Dad and I looked at Oscar, who hadn't moved a muscle.

"It's tradition, dude," I said.

He rolled his eyes and lifted his.

"To your mom!" Dad exclaimed. We clinked mugs. He brought the mug to his lips and chugged his nog. "Ha! *That's* how you start Christmas morning."

I took a big sip, swallowed, and exhaled loudly. "Ahhh. Wow. Strong."

Dad clasped my shoulder. "There's no other way to make it. Anything less wouldn't be worth it."

Oscar put his untouched mug in the sink and ran the water. *What a baby.*

"That's lame. The toast was to Mom."

He squinted. "I don't need to drink alcohol to honor my mother."

"You're so uptight. It's not about the alcohol. It's about Mom."

Dad poured himself another mugful. "Let it go. There's more for us." He raised his arm and then took a huge sip.

I turned my back on Oscar and high-fived Dad.

Oscar moped around all day, disappearing for long stretches of time. Dad had to call him down for Christmas dinner, and by that time, Dad was feeling no pain. The eggnog was long gone, and he was well into a bottle of wine.

Oscar asked if he could turn down the reggae as soon as he entered the kitchen. Dad didn't hear him. He was in his own world, dancing all around. I was already at the table grubbing on turkey, so I just watched.

The kitchen went quiet, and Dad froze over by the sink. "What'd you do that for?" he shouted.

"I asked if I could turn it down, Dad," Oscar said. He swallowed and blinked.

"Tha music mmmakes mmmeee happeee," Dad slurred. "Turn it onnnn."

"Maybe we should get you to bed," Oscar said. He locked eyes with me and lifted his brows, pleading.

"Relax. Let Dad eat. He needs to get some food into him," I said. I went back to my plate and shoved a huge forkful of mashed potatoes into my mouth.

Without a word, Oscar took his seat and helped himself to dinner.

Dad stumbled to the table and plopped into his chair. "*This* boy knows what I need." He squeezed my shoulder.

Oscar's cheeks flushed, and he dropped his eyes. I thought that would make my brother storm out, but he stayed.

He didn't make sense to me.

Why couldn't he ever let loose, laugh, have fun? I stared at him across the table. He never let me in. He was like a vault locked inside another vault, buried underneath tons of concrete.

It was kind of a bummer.

OSCAR

Peggy asks us to gather up anything that belongs to us or Dad. Vance and I put everything in our backpacks. I squash the urge to look at my last drawing of Dad and shove my sketchbook in.

"Come sit over here, boys." Peggy motions us to the sitting room. I take one end of the sofa, Vance the other. Peggy sits in the chair. "I found out that it *will* be the same social worker you met at the hospital. Ms. Becker. She's on her way. Don't quote me on this, but I think she's the best at what she does. I've seen a lot of social workers in this place, and she stands out. You will be in excellent hands."

All I can muster is a nod. Grief has rendered me a blob.

"When will someone come for our dad?" Vance whispers.

"The funeral home is on their way as well. We always suggest that family leave the room before their loved one is moved. Ms. Becker will meet you in the Common Room." Peggy stands. "You have your belongings?"

We mumble our yeses.

"I'll walk you both down," Peggy says.

Vance stands and I do the same. Peggy is already in the hall, waiting. My brother and I lock eyes. We know this is the end of seeing our father in a place where he was alive. Where he was breathing. Where he sighed, had a heartbeat.

I find my voice and tell Peggy we'll be out in a minute, and I close the door.

We mope and take up our usual positions around his bed. I rest my hand on Dad's forearm. The chill to his skin makes fresh tears erupt.

"Is he cold?" Vance asks.

I wipe tears with my free hand and nod.

Vance copies me and lays his hand on Dad's other arm. "Say hi to Mom. I'm going to miss you every day."

I choke into my elbow a few times and then sniffle. "I h-hope you're at peace, Dad." How will we walk out of this room? Leave our father behind? I don't know if I'm capable of releasing his arm. His skin. Him.

It's all too much.

There's a small comfort in knowing that Vance and I have lost all apprehension related to weeping in front of each other. Death strips pride from the living, which is a gift. But it wasn't like that with Mom. Back then, I never felt comfortable showing my true sorrow to Vance. I had my darkest moments alone.

I steal glances at my brother, trying to figure out what has changed. Is it me? Is it him? Are we just too broken to care?

There's a gentle knock on the door and Peggy says, "The funeral home people are here, boys."

Vance and I remove our hands at the same time and try to catch our breath. Both of us sound like sputtering engines. We grab our backpacks and walk toward the door.

Neither of us looks back.

VANCE

THREE MONTHS AGO

"Happy belated birthday, Vance," Mr. Richards said from across his desk.

My probation meetings were down to every other week, which I was psyched about. Otherwise, I would've been there *on* my actual birthday last Friday. Since I'd turned eighteen, Dad threw me a big party at the bar. He closed the restaurant section that night and had everything set up in there. I'm pretty sure the party was packed with lots of kids because they thought they could get wasted. Dad really only served jerk chicken sandwiches, fries, and cake—no alcohol. I was proud of him. He didn't even let anyone sneak a shot in the back.

Well, there was no alcohol for me and my friends, but *Dad* was three sheets by the end of the night. I had to drive home. But partygoers got high in the bathroom so they got over the lack of drinking real quick. A toked-up Growler stood on one of the tables and led the place—even the bar side—in a rowdy rendition of "Happy Birthday."

I smiled at Mr. Richards. "Thanks."

He stopped writing and looked over his glasses. "According to your clean urine, you stayed away from parties. Smart man, 'cause if you get yourself arrested now that you're eighteen, well, whole new ball game."

"My dad *did* throw me a huge party, alcohol-free of course." I put my hands behind my head. "How many times do I have to tell you… I'm not messing up anymore." My urge to party was sleeping. I just wanted to be done with this whole process so I could go back to planning for college. When I went to Drexel, the urge would awaken. I had no doubt about that. But even then I intended to reel it in a little so that I never ended up across from a probation officer again. I'd had enough.

Mr. Richards huffed. "If I had a dollar for every time I heard that, I'd be on a beach in Jamaica."

Even though I'd grown to like Mr. Richards, he was the type of guy who never lightened up. He wasn't a dick or anything. He was just all about probation. All the time. Even when I'd

K. M. Walton

try to get him talking about the Eagles—nope, he'd tell me we weren't there to talk sports and then change the subject back to me. I think I grew to respect his laser-focused dedication to his job. The guy should've won probation officer awards.

"We're closing in on the end, Vance." He shuffled a few papers. "I'll see you four more times, which takes us to the end of March."

"And then what happens?"

"Pretty simple. You stay out of trouble and live your life."

"I like the sound of that." We shook hands, and I headed to my car. I'd been driving myself for a while. Thank God. As I drove away, I pictured Oscar fist pumping when I'd told him he was fired from chauffeur duty. I'd been happy about that too. We never had too much to say to each other during the drives. We never had too much to say to each other during life.

Oscar was at my party, but he wasn't present. He spent most of the night bar-backing for Joey and Bill. I don't remember seeing his face when everyone sang to me, and I looked. He was probably out back sulking or drawing or staring into space.

I don't know how Oscar got home that night because he was already gone by the time Dad wanted to leave, so it was just me and Dad on the car ride home. I don't think Dad even noticed that Oscar wasn't in the car with us. But he had made it home. He was passed out on the sofa with his earbuds in. His sketchbook sat on the coffee table, taunting me.

Oscar kept his drawings private. He didn't even show Dad. I always wondered if he was any good. I'd seen some of his stuff over the years—the things he'd done in middle school art class—and I thought he was okay. Nothing jaw dropping. The way he kept it so secret made me think he was embarrassed by the dumb crap he drew and because he *wasn't* that good.

Criticism usually cut Oscar off at the knees. His backbone was made of Jell-O. I honestly had no idea how he would be able to function as an adult. Life could be shitty. People could be shitty. And there were lots of shitty people who said shitty things. What was he going to do, run away and hide in his room every time his feelings got hurt?

That wouldn't work.

Dad had already stumbled up to bed. I swear Oscar's sketchbook got all glowy, calling out: *Open me!* As slowly as I could, I slid it off the table. He didn't move a muscle. Mozart was probably blaring in his ears, which was perfect for me. I hustled into the dining room and used the flashlight on my phone.

The first few drawings were old. And just okay. There *were* no rainbows or sunrises. But as I turned the pages, his skills improved, a lot. The book was filled with sketches of people.

About midway through, I flipped the page and an uncanny sketch of my mother stared back at me. She was on the phone. She was clearly upset about something. I could see it on her face. In her eyes.

There was a drawing of me and Dad dancing in the kitchen. He had his favorite Red Stripe T-shirt on, and I wore my lacrosse uniform. My hair was matted and my cheeks flushed. I was sweaty from practice. And we looked so happy. Oscar captured the emotion and...wow...

I looked at every drawing. Many were of me and Dad. Some just Dad. But they were all good.

Oscar was good.

Holy crap. He was excellent.

OSCAR

We shuffle to the Common Room with our heads hung low. I toss my backpack onto the sofa and sit. My first move is to drop my head into my hands so that I can continue releasing the tears in private. I can only see Vance's feet as he walks toward the huge brown chair across from me. He leans his backpack against the side and sits as well.

For a while, the only sounds coming from us are sniffling, sobbing, coughing. I am oddly soothed by it. We're in our own grief bubble. Untouchable. Vance's pain is my pain—it glides through me with each moan. Light yet dense.

That stranger's moan suddenly comes to mind, and I'm dumbfounded at how similar we all sound. Maybe Death spends seconds in all of us, making a single harmony of sadness.

"H-how come you never showed D-dad your drawings?" Vance chokes out.

I lift my head. Vance is staring at me. *My drawings? Why does he care about my drawings all of a sudden?* "Why?"

He grabs a handful of tissues and cleans off his face before answering me. "Because he probably would've liked them."

My cheeks burn and my palms are warm. Hadn't he just been freaking out on me for sketching Dad? "How do you know if he would've liked them? He never seemed too interested in me or my life." I close my eyes and drop my chin. My father just died, and I'm already finding the negative. I am disgusting.

"Because I know."

My gaze lifts. "Because you know *how*?"

Vance's breathing quickens. He's clearly nervous, which can mean only one thing: he defied me and looked in my sketchbook.

"The night of my birthday party, when Dad and I got home and you were asleep on the sofa with your earbuds in, you left your sketchbook out on the coffee table."

I remember waking up in a panic the next morning, seeing it just sitting there, out in the open. Leaving it out was something I'd never done before. My drawings were part of my soul. And my soul was private. Instead of confronting my brother or Dad at breakfast that day, I chose to bundle up against the cold January morning and walk. I had my sketchbook tucked underneath my arm and pencils in my back pocket. I walked to the park a few blocks away, sat on one of the swings, and drew Mom's furry snow boots from memory. If my lips hadn't frozen, I probably would've stayed there till dark and continued drawing her things.

"You had no right to open it, Vance," I say with zero verve. Even though I feel violated, the fight is gone in me. I am like a half-dead September bee.

He nods. "I know. But I'm not sorry I did it. That sketch you did of Mom on the phone is…" He pauses. "It's so real."

My eyes fill and I look away. That is the first time my brother has complimented me.

"Will you show me the one you just did of Dad? Please?" he asks.

I remain still for a while. I'm trying to make sense of where I am, what I'm doing, what I want to do. My father is gone. My brother is all I have left in this world. I look to him, and he's staring at me.

It's my turn to wipe away the tears. I clear my throat. "Do you know that you're the only human being on earth who I can say, 'Do you remember when Dad…?' The only one."

"Same for me with you."

K. M. Walton

We let that depressing revelation sit and fill the room for a while. In short, we are all the other has left.

Vance stretches out his legs and asks again to see the new sketch of Dad.

His venom seems at bay and his desire genuine. And he has already seen eighty percent of the book, albeit under dishonest circumstances. One cannot *un*see something. I take in a huge breath and reach for my backpack. With trembling hands, I place the book on the coffee table and slide it toward him. "I'd rather not be in the room when you open it. It would be too much for me to handle."

I stand and walk down the other hall, the hall away from my father's room.

VANCE

MARCH HAD BEEN SIMULTANEOUSLY FANTASTIC AND SHITTY. Fantastic in that I officially finished up with Mr. Richards *and* rehab, like, within a week of each other. Dad took me and Oscar out to dinner in town to celebrate, and we actually had a decent time. My brother wasn't a moody a-hole, and Dad didn't get trashed until we got back home. We were winners all around that night.

The winning didn't last long. Don't forget, March had also been pretty shitty. I went to my first lacrosse practice and really struggled. My trainer told me to expect it so I didn't freak then. But when I went to my second, third, fourth, and fifth practice, and it didn't get any easier?

FREAKING OUT.

It was during my fifth and last practice that I pulled my grafted hamstring, pulled as in I couldn't stand, and the pain was so effed up that I almost passed out. As soon as I got home, my knee blew up like a balloon and I punched a hole in my bedroom wall. Went straight through the drywall.

Five days passed, and as I crutched through the halls of school—each step very painful—I knew what I had to do. Drexel had to be told about my injury. If I couldn't make it through high school practices, there was no way in hell I'd be able to play college Level I.

I didn't ask for anyone's opinions, even Dad's, because hearing people try to talk me out of it would only make me sicker about it. Dad told every single person who sat at the bar that his oldest got a full lacrosse scholarship to Drexel University. He would definitely tell me to suck it up and give it a go.

I couldn't do it.

My knee never regained full extension, and my trainer, while optimistic, was a hard-core realist. He was the one who flat-out said the likelihood of me playing Level I was slim to none. I really thought I could beast through it all and come out stronger than I was before. I thought I could at least play for my high school team.

My hand shook as I dialed Coach's cell. I thought I'd start with my high school coach and then work my way up to Drexel. "Coach? It's Vance. Yeah, I'm doing my best to take it easy. I know. But yeah, so the reason I'm calling is to let you know that I can't finish the season. Yeah, it's my knee. It, uh, isn't right. Uh-huh, lots of pain." After an uncomfortable silence I said, "Coach? You still there? Okay, so that's it. I'm really sorry. Uh-huh, right. Yeah, I'm calling Drexel next. I know, it'll be very rough letting that go. Thanks. See you around. Bye."

K. M. Walton

OSCAR

MY LEGS FALL ASLEEP FROM SITTING ON THE TOILET FOR so long. A bathroom stall is the only place I could think of where I'd have quiet and privacy. No one has come in yet, and I've been in here for at least fifteen minutes.

I stand and stretch. Vance has probably seen every sketch by now. Even though I technically didn't use the bathroom, I still wash my hands. As I round the corner, I smash full force into Jacque Beaufort. I bite my tongue. She squeaks and grabs the metal railing that lines both sides of every hall.

We stand panting for a few seconds. I'm shifting my tongue around in my mouth, trying to make the pain stop. I'm definitely bleeding.

Jacque drops her chin and takes in a few deep breaths through her nose. She stares at the floor and whispers, "Oscar, I'm so sorry about your dad."

Right away, I wish that she'd looked me in the eye and said that. I wanted to see her face.

Without thinking, without an ounce of hesitation, I reach out and gently lift her chin. Her mouth falls open, and her eyes go wide. It is safe to say that I've stunned us both.

Maybe it's the fact that I'm bleeding.

Maybe it's because I'm in a grief stupor.

Maybe it's a residual effect of my brother's compliment.

I honestly am unsure. But I did it. We are currently staring at each other, and my hand remains underneath her chin. "Could you say that one more time?" I ask.

Her chest rises and falls, and a tear glides down her beautiful face. She nods. "I'm so sorry about your dad."

I swallow my tinny spit. "My name. You forgot to say my name." Hearing my name leave her mouth while I'm touching her just might qualify as the most sensual moment of my life to date.

She gently places her hand on my extended forearm. A jolt of God-knows-what goes directly from my arm to my crotch. Every skin cell registers this bombshell touch. *Please, not now!* I'm afraid to look down.

Jacque draws her bottom lip in before saying, "Oscar, I am incredibly sorry about your dad."

Why does this overwhelmingly intimate moment have to happen mere hours after the loss of my father? Guilt draws my hand away. I look down. It's flat. I cross my arms tightly. I fight the urge to pinch underneath my armpits as punishment. The only thing stopping me is the fear of Jacque seeing the ridiculous pain-face I'd make. "Thank you." I somehow manage a small smile.

Again, I'm rendered speechless at this moment.

Her face wrinkles with concern. "You're bleeding!"

I swallow and wish I had some water to swish around in my mouth. After swiping my chin, I can see that I'm blood-free. Thank God.

Jacque turns and runs away.

Now *this* feels like a normal situation to me.

VANCE

ONE MONTH AGO

"This is the kind of thing you discuss with a parent, Vance. For God's sake!" my father yelled from behind the bar. We were alone. Joey and Bill weren't there yet, and Oscar had to stay after school to finish some project. I'd planned to drop the bomb when it was just the two of us.

I knew he'd flip out when I told him about Drexel, but not this bad. For a minute there, I thought he might finally hit me. I was too nervous to sit down so I decided to pace.

"So now what, genius?" he shouted. "It's too late to apply somewhere else!"

My feet took me to the other end of the bar.

"You just, poof, gave up a full ride," he snapped. "So you had a few rough practices. That doesn't mean you give up everything you've worked for! Without even talking with your father."

A few rough practices? Was he really that clueless? And last time I checked, it was my knee, not his. Was he the one who had to look himself in the mirror and know, deep down in his gut, that he'd ruined his life? Did he have to do that?

He could walk and run and jump without pain. Without wincing and grinding his teeth. *He* didn't have a gnawing fear that wrapped itself around his confidence, squeezing the life out of it until it was nothing but an empty shell—fear of reinjury.

Fear of the volcanic pain.

Dad smacked the bar. "Will you stand still and stop walking around like an idiot?"

I turned to face him. "Don't you think I'd have taken the scholarship if I could? Do you seriously think I *wanted* to stop playing lacrosse?" I pounded my chest a few times. "Can you see me, Dad? I fucked up everything, just like you said!"

Dad's shoulders slumped. He was panting and white as a ghost. *Holy shit, was he having a heart attack?* "Are you all right?" I marched behind the bar. He waved me off and went into his office. Of course I followed him. "Dad! Stop."

He sat at his desk and glared at me. The color was back in his cheeks.

"I did what I had to do. I didn't have a choice," I said. Saying it out loud confirmed my decision. My knee would never be the same.

His lips formed a thin line, and he shook his head. "I am your damn father, Vance. I deserved to be told. Now get out and stack the cases."

Before closing his door, I turned and said, "Just so you know, I have a plan, Dad."

OSCAR

Jacque Beaufort and I just shared an actual moment.

My body unfreezes from shock and I start moving, while Jacque bolts toward me holding a water bottle out in front of her. She comes to a stop, grabs my hand, and places the cold bottle in it. If the sparks I feel were true electricity, we'd both be smoldering piles of flesh on the carpet.

"For your m-mouth," she pants.

I look down and she's still touching me.

She jerks her hand away. "Sorry."

"Thank you." I have never looked at another human being with more intensity than I'm doing right now. Red-hot laser beams must be shooting from my eyes.

"You're welcome." A nervous smile dances across her face. "Do you guys need anything? Can I get either of you anything?"

I shake my head and try my best to catch my breath. I'm not entirely certain this whole thing isn't taking place in an alternate universe, and the real me is still sitting on that toilet waiting for the right time to emerge and face the dark clouds.

"I think someone may be here to see you and Vance," she says. "I saw him talking to a woman in the Common Room. Do you have a curly-haired aunt?"

The social worker.

I don't want to move from this spot. Moving means facing my father's death head on.

Before I can answer her, Jacque says, "I wish I could say something to make you feel better. I'm so sorry. I know I already said that, but I mean it."

We stare, our gazes locked.

She breaks the silence. "I gotta go. The nurses get mad if I'm in one place for too long." She rocks on her heels once before walking away.

"Thank you," I say after she's gone, wishing I'd said it to her face. I twist open the water and guzzle half of it. The cold feels glorious on my tongue. As soon as I swallow, the stinging registers in my brain. "Owww."

K. M. Walton

A terrible yet simple thought forms: *My father will never sip cool water again.*

Sorrow erupts in my heart, melting me from the inside.

VANCE

THREE WEEKS AGO

Dad still hadn't asked about my plan. He was too busy being pissed off at me. We hadn't had a decent exchange since I told him about Drexel. It was mostly him barking orders at me at the bar or asking me to pass something to him at the dinner table. For the first time in my life, it was like he had nothing to talk about with me.

Dad and I were never at a loss for words. That was Oscar's territory. There could be no doubt that we were tight. There was a connection. We had stuff in common. How long was he going to drag this shit out?

You can't just unravel a father-son relationship.

Right?

I'd tried putting on his favorite songs, getting dinner started before he got home, asking questions about the date he went on, the new beer tap at the bar, the friggin' weather. Nothing worked.

We'd just finished another uncomfortable dinner. My steak burrito sat like a boulder in my gut. He disappeared into the living room, and then while Oscar and I were cleaning up the dishes, he came in and announced, "I'm going out for a drink. Don't wait up."

He slammed the front door and sped down the street.

Oscar said, "Why didn't you just talk to him first? Before you called Drexel."

I spun around. "It's none of your business!" My brother was right. I should've told Dad. I messed up. Of course I'd never admit that to Oscar.

He tossed his head side to side. "There's so much anger inside you. So much," he said under his breath. He balled his fists and his voice rose. "But guess what? We're all Dad has left! Have you forgotten that fact? Huh? And while the two of you try to out-selfish each other, neither of you have given an ounce of thought to the reality that we—the three of us—are a family, and families are supposed to be there for each other, look out for each other, *not* keep secrets like dropping full scholarships from each other.

"Families should feel like safety and home and love. Not this family though. Oh no, *here* we have anger and insults and lies and pain. That's what *we* have. So how can you expect Dad to react any other way to your little bombshell? He's not capable, Vance! We're about as messed up as any family can be." Oscar's chest heaved.

I'd never seen him so fired up. I'd never heard him say so many sentences in a row.

Every word he said was true. We were a mess. "What is today, all gang up on Vance day?"

"Oh, that's right. The world revolves around Vance. I forgot." Oscar slammed the frying pan into the cabinet.

"You know what? In *Oscarland*, with its fancy classical music and secret drawings and constant 'no one understands me' bullshit, the world revolves around *you*! How many times did you drive me to physical therapy? Twenty? Thirty? A friggin' million? And during those drives, how many times did you ask about my pain? About my progress? About me? I know how many times! Zero! Not once. You were too busy being lost in sad little Oscarland. Well, guess what, asshole, you're no picnic for a brother either!"

If only I had my phone on me to capture the look on Oscar's

stupid face. It was a mixture of constipation and amazement. We stared at each other for what felt like years. We'd said more to each other in the past two minutes than we had in the past two years. The kitchen was full of words.

Oscar's eyes got glassy. "Oscarland? That's what you call my life? Like it's an amusement park. You and Dad, all you do is make assumptions about me. I'm weird because I like classical music. I'm weird because I'm not into sports. I'm weird because I'm quiet. You don't know me. Neither does Dad."

My brother gave me no chance to respond before he stomped up to his room. *Good.* I wouldn't have had a response anyway because he was right.

OSCAR

I HEAD TO THE COMMON ROOM. IT *IS* MS. BECKER, THE
social worker. When I approach, she requests that Vance and
I sit with our backs to the hallway. When Vance asks her why,
she says facing the window is less distracting. I close my eyes.
She doesn't want us to catch a glimpse of them wheeling our
father's body out. I get it.

She reaches into her briefcase and pulls out a folder. It has
our last name across the tab. Vance digs through his backpack
and lifts out a legal-sized, white envelope and places it in front
of him. "His will." He slides it across the table.

Ms. Becker doesn't look down; she looks at us. "First, let me
say I am very, very sorry for your loss, boys. I know meeting
with me is the last thing you want to do, but I've found that

the quicker I get things started on my end, the better it is for my clients. I'm your advocate, and it's my job to make sure the right decisions are made concerning your futures."

"I don't want to talk about my *future*! I can't think about that right now," Vance barks.

Ms. Becker nods, unfazed. "You're absolutely right, Vance. Let me back up. Let's start with your father." She pulls papers from the envelope and lays them out. Neither Vance nor I have actually seen Dad's will. What if he says we have to move to Alaska with our grandparents or ship off to Singapore with Aunt Renee? Ms. Becker carefully scours the document, and I am about to shatter with a hideous mixture of heartache and anxiety. My fingers tingle and my stomach tightens.

"Your father requested a private service and burial. That takes a tremendous amount of pressure off you guys. I will definitely help you navigate through the process, and if you like, I can be your liaison with the funeral director."

We nod, almost in unison.

She stares down at the will. "He left everything to you both, fifty-fifty. And he clearly had faith in you, Vance. He spells out very clearly that you are to get custody of Oscar in the event of his death."

The world shifts around me. Or maybe I moved. I am blurred. *Vance will have* custody *of me?* We can't even discuss what's for dinner without animosity. And he will be in charge?

Vance fidgets in his seat. "Does that mean—" He stops.

Ms. Becker looks him square in the eye. "It means that until Oscar turns eighteen in November, you will be his legal guardian."

We are stunned. We are silent. We are frozen.

"However, Vance, you do have some choices. And I'd be happy to go through them in a few days, maybe after the funeral?"

Despite feeling slightly numb at the moment, *I* want to hear Vance's choices. "Go over them now," I say. "Please."

Her eyes dart from mine to Vance's. "Are you sure?"

My brother turns to me. "I'm ready."

VANCE

THREE WEEKS AGO

MY CELL RANG, WAKING ME UP. IT WAS THREE IN THE morning. "Hello?"

"Hello?" a female voice said.

"Who's this?"

"This is Ms. Becker, hospital social worker at West Chester Hospital. Your father has been in a car accident, and we're trying to stabilize him. Is there any way you can come to the hospital?"

The lady's voice was so calm. There was no panic or sense of urgency. I sat up, and when I tried to speak, only a croak came out. I cleared my throat. "Wait, wait. Are you serious?"

"Yes, I'm serious. May I ask how old you are?"

Air shot from my nose. "Eighteen. Is he gonna be all right?"

"You and your family drive safely. Come to the main ER desk, and I'll take you—"

I hung up on her and raced into Oscar's room. "Oscar?" I shook him wildly.

"What the hell are you doing?" He shoved my hands away.

"It's Dad! He's in the emergency room. Some lady just called and said he was in a car accident. They want us there right now!"

Oscar pushed himself up to sitting. "Oh my God."

"Get dressed. Let's go!"

I pulled up to the emergency room doors and parked. The security guard stopped us. "Are either of you the patient?"

"No. Our dad's in there!" I barked.

"I'm sorry, guys, but you can't park there. You're in the ambulance lane. The ER lot is right over—"

I cut him off. "Seriously, sir? Our father could be dying right now." I turned and went through the automatic doors.

Oscar grabbed my arm. "We can't block the ambulances, Vance!"

"I don't give a shit about ambulances!" I screamed in his face.

He held out his hand. "Give me the keys."

I bit the inside of my cheek to stop from bawling right there in front of the guard and dropped the keys into his palm. I turned and darted to the front desk.

The nurse called someone as soon as I asked where Steve Irving was. A blond, curly-haired woman came through the double doors. She introduced herself as the woman from the phone as we walked double time through the ER. She pulled a curtain back and there he was. My knees buckled. "Oh shit, Dad. What did you do?" He was unconscious. Cuts all over his face, hands, and forearms. He had some type of breathing apparatus with tubes and straps, and he had a baby-blue neck brace on.

The front desk nurse brought Oscar back. He was panting. "I ran," he whispered to no one.

We stood shoulder to shoulder and stared at our broken father.

One sentence was on repeat in my head: *He might die mad at me.*

OSCAR

Ms. Becker shakes a few curls off her face and then takes a deep breath. "Okay. Options. Vance, I assume you're headed off to college in the fall?"

My brother and I steal a look before he responds. "Well, it's complicated," he says.

She grins. "Complicated is my specialty."

"I have a plan," he says and then stops.

Ms. Becker and I wait.

Vance buries his face in his hands and loses it.

Ms. Becker and I wait.

Crying doesn't faze her. I like that. Truthfully, at this point, crying doesn't faze me either—even when Vance does it. So we let him get it out. I stare out the window over Ms. Becker's shoulder, and she begins to fill out papers. It's all very patient, very civilized.

He grabs the box of tissues and mops off. "That was one of the last things I said to my dad. I never got to tell h-him…" He's unable to finish.

Ms. Becker says, "I know this is rough. Do you need a few more minutes?"

"No." Vance blows his nose. "I'm good."

"There is no rush. I can wait," she says.

He shakes his head. "College. Yeah. Complicated. I lost my full ride to Drexel on account of blowing out my knee. I played lacrosse. My big plan was to commute and take a few classes at Drexel, not go full time, get them under my belt, and then maybe my knee would get stronger, and I don't know, maybe I could get my scholarship back." He sighs. "Now that I say it out loud, it sounds pretty stupid. Without the scholarship, Dad said I had to pay for college on my own. I don't even know what I want to major in. My whole world was lacrosse. It's all stupid."

Ms. Becker tilts her head and smiles. "Stupid? That was the exact path *I* took after graduating from high school. Applied late, took some classes at West Chester University, got in as a full-time student, had no clue what I wanted to study, remained undecided for a whole year. Don't be so hard on yourself, Vance. You've got a lot on your plate right now."

Ever since Vance's surgery, he's been different. Not like, whoa, Vance is suddenly volunteering at the homeless shelter and being kind to everyone. It has been a subtle, quiet difference. Actually, *he* was quieter. His anger still bubbled just below the surface, but it was like his voice and his overt aggression were yanked down a level. I steal side-eyed glances at my brother. I think Ms. Becker is right. Vance *has* been rough on himself.

I simply failed to notice.

A thin string of regret ties around my heart. And tightens.

Ms. Becker thumbs through Dad's will. "According to this document, you both have college funds. Looks like each account has one hundred and fifty thousand in it."

My eyebrows pinch together. *One hundred and fifty thousand dollars? Each?* Why hadn't Dad told us he'd put away so much? Was he planning on surprising us or something?

"W-what did you say?" Vance sputters.

She tucks a curl behind her ear. "I'm guessing from your reactions that you were unaware these accounts existed."

"No, we knew about them. I had no idea they contained that much," Vance says. He turns to me. "Did you know?"

I mouth, "No."

She says, "Well, if I've learned anything doing this job for the past ten years, it's that parents are mysterious creatures. Sometimes in a good way. Sometimes not so much."

"This is a good way, right? I mean, one hundred and fifty thousand dollars for each of us? That's unreal. Why didn't he tell us?" Vance rambles.

"I'm sure he had his reasons," she says.

Vance and I lock eyes, and he repeats, "This is...unreal..."

"Agreed," I say.

Ms. Becker brings our attention back to Vance's options. "So, you don't *have* to be Oscar's legal guardian. He turns eighteen"—she shuffles through papers—"in November, which is only seven months away. If you decide you want to go *away* to college, like, full time, Vance, especially now that you can pay for it, we can place Oscar with foster parents." She turns and looks at me. "I don't mean to speak of you like you're not sitting directly in front of me, Oscar. I apologize. This is your life as well."

"Did you say foster parents?" Vance asks.

I answer for her. "She did."

"Like, he would have to live with strangers for seven months? In their house?" he clarifies.

"Yes, that's how foster care works. But I know of an incredible couple here in Chester County. They live on three acres with a pond *and* a barn. They are wonderful people. They've been foster parents for fifteen years. Kids lucky enough be placed with them keep in touch. They take a Christmas card photo in front of the pond every year with the children they've fostered. I think they're up to twenty, maybe twenty five. And they have space. Right now."

VANCE

THREE WEEKS AGO

"Is your mom parking?" Ms. Becker asked.

Oscar's eyes bulged. I had to grasp the side of the bed to steady myself. "She's dead. She died in a car accident," I said.

"She was in the car?" she said.

Oscar said without turning around to look at her, "Our mom died three years ago, ma'am. She's not parking the car."

"Oh, boys. I'm sorry. I'm so sorry." She slipped behind the curtain and apologized again before walking away.

Hearing Oscar say it out loud, that Mom died in a car accident, was like one of those cartoon anvils landing on my head: Both parents had horrible car accidents? Was the

Universe jabbing at me with its pointy stick? What are you going to do about it, Vance, huh? Huh?

A young female doctor in a white lab coat pulled back the curtain. Her red hair was back in a ponytail, her very serious face covered in freckles. "Are you his sons?"

We nodded.

"Your father is in critical condition. The paramedics on the scene actually brought him back to life. He had stopped breathing."

"Is he going to be okay?" I asked.

She pressed her lips together. "We're doing everything we can to save his life."

Just then, Ms. Becker was at her side. She said something to the doctor and then waved us out to the hall. "My office is right over there." She pointed straight ahead. "We need to talk, and I'd like to do that in private. I promise it won't take long."

"I'm not leaving Dad," I said.

"I understand. Then we can talk in there." She held up the curtain, and the three of us were back at Dad's side.

I honestly had no idea what she said. I zoned out as terrifying thought after terrifying thought bounced around inside my skull. My dad had to live. He didn't have a choice. We needed him; it was that simple. I didn't get to say goodbye. He was too young to die. We would be orphans.

And on and on and on.

Oscar tapped my arm. "Does Dad have a will?"

I whipped around. "A will? Why?" I screeched.

Ms. Becker tucked her hair behind her ear. "I understand this is an extremely difficult situation, but it's an important bit of information for me to know."

Her voice was so calm, just like on the phone. Each word she said lowered my anxiety. I took a few deep breaths to clear my head. "He has two—a living will and a regular one. He showed me the sealed envelopes and made me watch where he put them. They're in the bottom drawer of his dresser underneath his jeans." I didn't want to look at Oscar. I couldn't take his wounded expression. Dad telling *me* about the wills and showing *me* where they were kept was one more thing for him to feed the isolation monster living inside him.

My thoughts and worries swallowed me up. White noise was all that registered. Was the lady talking again? I couldn't be sure. I stared at my dad.

"Based on your father's present condition, a living will is a good thing. It'll spell out his medical wishes. And, Vance, since you *are* eighteen, you are legally an adult. You *could* be appointed as your brother's guardian in the event of your father's death, assuming of course other plans aren't spelled out in his will. However, we'll cross that bridge when we come to it."

One word pierced through my haze: death. I whipped around. "Did you say death?"

"Yes, you *could* be appointed as your brother's guardian in the event of your father's death," she said.

Kaboom. "What?" I shouted. "You're talking about his *death*? What kind of messed-up shit is going on? He's right there...breathing!"

She took a step back.

I flung open the curtain and jogged down the hall.

OSCAR

Vance, Ms. Becker, and I sit in silence for a few minutes. She doesn't find the need to fill the quiet moments with chatter or questions—I like that. She lets things unfold as they may without forcing the situation.

Vance folds his hands in front of him. He looks so serious. "So if I *don't* go away to college, then Oscar can stay home?"

I slowly turn my head to look at my brother. If words could leave my brain and crawl from my ears, these are the words you'd see scuttling down my arms to make themselves part of the world: *respect* and *love*. These are not insignificant words. They are colossal. Their weight would crash them through the floor, through the foundation, through the ground. They would be forced to reassemble in the center of the earth.

That's how massive these words are that are coming from my head.

All those nights I'd laid awake wondering if my brother loved me, concluding the answer to be no.

I was wrong.

I was as wrong as any brother could be.

In fact, I was dead wrong.

Ms. Becker nods. "Yes. But if you do move forward with legal guardianship, we don't just pat you on the head and tell you to have good lives. There are procedures in place for your protection. There would be biweekly visits from a Children's Protective Services social worker. He or she would be making sure you guys are handling your new life, that you're safe and taking care of yourselves properly."

"They can come check on us every day if they want to," Vance says.

Ms. Becker raises one eyebrow and smiles. "Listen, you don't have to make this decision today, Vance. I can give—"

Vance interrupts her. "Decision's made. He's not going off to live on a farm with twenty-five kids. Pond or no friggin' pond. And he's not going to be on a stranger's Christmas card. He's going to live in *our* house, sleep in *his* bed, watch *his* TV." He turns to me. "You cool with that?"

I roll my eyes. "That's kind of a ridiculous question." As

soon as I say it, I want to take it back. My stomach coils. I actually don't know what to say here.

Vance slowly nods and kind of looks through me. I'm not sure if he heard my smart-mouthed response. There's something going on inside his head. "We had an ultimatum, didn't we? Go our separate ways, do our own thing…" His jaw tightens, and he rubs the back of his neck. "We owe it to Mom and Dad to take care of each other."

My mouth falls open.

What kind of day am I living? Nothing feels normal.

"Right?" Vance asks me. "They're expecting us to. I can feel it."

Ms. Becker's eyes light up. "Death can sometimes kill a family." Her head bobs. "Other times a rebirth occurs. Like now. It's special to see—and one of the reasons I love my job."

Vance gives her a little smile, nods, and turns to me. "We can't mess up anymore, Oscar. With each other. We have to make this work."

An actual warm feeling flushes throughout my body. Is this what happiness feels like? Love maybe? Understanding? Who knows. My words are melting before they form, the temperature of this joy too hot. But I want my brother to know I've heard him, that I agree, so I lock eyes and nod. Over and over and over.

VANCE

TEN DAYS AGO

Dad actually woke up the day after I'd freaked on the social worker. The doctor said he was lucky to be alive. She also made it very clear that his liver was very fragile, and if he drank, he'd die. That simple.

When we got home from school, our routine was to go check on Dad upstairs.

Dad raised a beer can in the air from his bed. "Cheers!" He guzzled a long sip and then wiped his chin with the back of his hand.

"Again?" Oscar whispered.

"This has to stop, Dad. Beer is just as bad as the hard

stuff! Look at your skin. It's the color of piss! You can't do this every day. You heard the doctor." I scolded him like a child.

"It's none of your damned business! Neither one of you," Dad shouted from his bed. Oscar and I stood at the foot. We were scared, but we'd never admit that to each other. I just *knew* we were. I could tell by the look in my brother's eyes. And I hadn't slept through the night since Dad was released from the hospital.

Oscar took a big breath. "The doctor was pretty adamant, Dad. She said no matter what you drink, you run the risk of complete liver failure. You were sitting up. You were awake. We all heard her say it. If you drink, you die." He sounded a little whiny. I knew it would set Dad off.

Dad was wasted—his sixth day in a row pounding beer. Empty cans littered the floor. I kicked one across the room, and it crashed against his dresser. "So you *want* to die? Is that it?" I turned on my heels and walked down the hall. Truly, I didn't want to hear his answer. It would be some drunk lie. Alcohol liked to eat the truth. It stuffed itself on honesty until it couldn't hold any more.

And then it puked all over your legs.

Down in the kitchen, I slammed as many cabinets as I could. It was very satisfying.

"I'm getting rid of all the alcohol in the house," Oscar announced as soon as he came down.

I gripped the counter and closed my eyes. We both knew Dad had friends, ways, and schemes to get more alcohol. Sure, we could pour every drop in the backyard, but he'd get more. The only bone he broke—miraculously—was his nose, so there was nothing stopping him from slowly walking down the stairs, getting into his car (even though his license was suspended), and driving to the bar—the bar he owned, the bar currently stocked with enough alcohol to get a neighborhood trashed—and drinking as much as he wanted.

He needed to be locked in a safe place. "He needs to be in rehab."

Oscar actually laughed for, like, a minute.

I fought the urge to tackle him to the floor. "You're *laughing*, you dick?"

He coughed and calmed down. "I can already tell you how that'll go, which I'm sure you don't need to hear. He's your father too."

"Oh, so your big idea is to piss him off by pouring out his bottles?"

The thought of losing him shoved its way inside my head again. As soon as he woke up in the hospital and stabilized, the reality of him dying drifted far, far away. He was alive and alert. He was talking and laughing. He wasn't dying.

But then his doctor came in and wanted to talk. Her talk was crystal clear: you drink, your already weak liver crashes and burns—but she said it with fancy medical words like cirrhosis and scar tissue. I went home that night and googled everything I could on liver failure. I'd tossed and turned till morning.

Dad's liver doctor appointment was tomorrow after school. What did he think that guy was going say to him? "So I see from your blood work and the lemony-yellow tone to your skin that you've been trashed. Well done, sir." No, the doctor was going to freak.

"That's it!" I shouted to myself. "The doctor can admit him to rehab! Doctors can do that. Like, just send people straight there if they need it."

Oscar's face pinched and he shook his head. "No, that's not how it works. Dad's an adult."

"I wasn't asking your friggin' opinion!" I smacked the cabinet door as hard as I could. Twice. My palm stung so I clenched and released a few times.

And then I whacked it again, and again, and again.

And again.

OSCAR

I STAND IN DAD'S BEDROOM DOORWAY. HIS BED REMAINS unmade but the cans are gone. I didn't clean them up. Did Vance? I can still see Dad lying there holding up his beer, defiantly saying, "Cheers!" He fell into a coma that next afternoon. He never made it to the liver doctor.

Vance and I found him unconscious in his bed when we got home from school. We called 911, and he spent a short time in the hospital before they moved him to the hospice.

His service is in two hours. It's only going to be me, Vance, Joey, and Bill.

Once the cell company released Dad's PIN, we got into his phone and called our grandparents and aunt.

My grandparents couldn't make it from Alaska. My aunt

couldn't make it from Singapore. Vance and I seriously didn't care if they came or not. They were just people. At first we didn't even want Joey and Bill to come, but then Vance made a good point—he said Dad would've wanted them there. He was right. They liked Dad, and Dad liked them. They'd stuck by him.

Ms. Becker really is our liaison with the funeral home. She calls each morning with a list of questions for me and Vance. We put her on speaker and answer them, together.

- No, we don't want to speak at the service.
- No, flowers are a waste of money.
- No, we don't practice any kind of religion.
- No, we don't want a memory book or funeral cards made.
- No, we don't plan to bring photo boards.
- Yes, we want Dad's coffin to be nice.
- Yes, we want his burial to happen right after.
- No, we don't want a limo. Vance can drive us. We know the way. It's the same cemetery as for Mom.

The Child Protective Services woman comes tomorrow morning. Ms. Becker says she is her favorite CPS social worker. We'll see.

"Eggs are ready," Vance yells up the stairs.

"Coming." I close Dad's door until it clicks. Of course we'll have to open it, maybe even when we get home, but there is the tiniest comfort in shutting his things away for the time being. A temporary break from *one* space in which he lived.

Vance and Growler sit at the table, already eating breakfast. It was my idea to invite Growler over last night. I thought he'd be the perfect person to hang out with. Vance objected at first, saying he wasn't ready to see people. I reminded him that it would be nice for *Growler* since he wasn't invited to Dad's service. Growler loved Dad. And besides, we still had the sunglasses he'd left at the hospice.

Vance texted him, and he got permission to sleep over. We hung out in the living room telling Dad story after Dad story. It was during one of those stories that I had a mini-revelation. The fact that I insisted on calling Growler "Stephen" was annoying. Growler was Growler, and that was that. The only reason I did it was to annoy Vance. I'd moved on from that.

The kitchen smells of melted butter and toast. "Looks good. Thanks." Complimenting Vance, showing him gratitude, still feels awkward, the words clunky in my mouth.

Vance drops his eyes. "Sure."

We trip over the exchange. We are unsure. We are in strange territory.

"*Tasted* good," Growler says. "I gotta bolt. My dad's expecting me to help with the garage cleanout, which starts in ten minutes. I'll be thinking of you guys today." He lifts his half-empty OJ glass. "To your dad!"

Vance and I raise our glasses, and the three of us clink. Growler simultaneously squeezes both of our shoulders before leaving.

We eat in silence. The seriousness of the day is all-powerful.

I cannot count the number of glances I take at our father's empty chair. Hundreds maybe. Despite my efforts at being subtle, Vance says, "Maybe we can start eating in the dining room."

I shrug and blink rapidly. The tears can't come yet.

He says, "You know how Dad loved Cliff's 'Many Rivers to Cross'?"

My hand trembles as I take a bite of eggs, and I nod.

"What if we play it on my phone and put it up to Dad's ear? Before Joey and Bill get there. Do you think he could really hear it?"

Who is this person sitting across from me? Will he retreat into his old personality soon? How long will Vance, the actual brother, be present and accounted for?

Vance answers his own question. "Probably not, right? I guess it would be more for us than him, wouldn't it? It's stupid." He stands and clears his plate from the table.

"It's not stupid."

He turns around. He's biting his cheek.

I point to Dad's empty chair. "How do we know where his soul is? What if he's here?" My voice rises. "What if he's sitting there, listening to us, screaming that he *wants* you to play the song? How do we know anything anymore, Vance? I don't know shit! I just don't know shit!" I pound the table with my fist. My fork jumps from my plate and rattles around.

Vance wipes a tear away. "I don't know shit either."

We silently clear the table and pack the dishwasher. I walk into the living room and plop down onto the sofa. Vance follows—again, this is new because he usually would be anywhere I *wasn't*.

"That picture…" he says, his voice drifting off.

What picture? Is he talking about one of my drawings?

He walks to the corner table, grabs the framed family photo from the zoo, and holds it up. "Let's bring this with us to Dad's thing. Mom loved this picture."

"Do you think they stopped loving each other?"

Without hesitation Vance says, "No."

I don't know where his certainty is coming from, and I'm not sure he's right, but it feels so good to hear it.

VANCE

TWO DAYS AGO

CALLING OSCAR A DICK *AND* AN ASSHOLE STUCK TO ME
for some reason. I couldn't erase the hurt look on his face.
Despite multiple instances of me trying to forget it, blow it
off, tell myself it was no big deal, I couldn't shake the guilt.

Guilt was new for me.

When Dad crumbled and landed in the hospice, I had lots
of time to wrestle with this new feeling, and I had no idea
what to do with it.

Oscar was still sitting in the empty stands over there. I
squinted to see who was running around the track. Just some
mom, nobody I knew. I headed back into the hospice. Waiting

for my brother to return wasn't something I'd do. We did our own thing.

I took my seat next to Dad's bed and immediately started counting his breaths. For three minutes in a row I only counted four breaths per minute. Only four. I was outside for barely five minutes, and he was down a breath. The nurse, I had to tell her. She was still sitting just outside the door at the mobile nurse's cart. "Excuse me?" I said.

She looked up, her expression kind. "Yes?"

"My dad's breaths are down to four a minute."

She stood and motioned me back into his room. After checking him out, she said, "It's a step closer. But I'd say he's still a day, maybe a day and a half away from passing. I'm sure you're not fond of our saying this, but it's true—he'll go when he's ready."

"Could it be sooner though?" My stomach knotted as the question left my mouth.

She nodded as she answered me. "Maybe. Again, I'm sorry for my wishy-washy answers. This place and our patients don't follow a regular time frame, which can be difficult for the families."

She asked if I needed anything, and when I told her no, she left me be. One of Dad's loud and startling breaths made my body jump. I wanted to go get Oscar, just in case. I grabbed my backpack and told the nurse I was going to bring my brother back inside. As soon as my feet hit the blacktop, I beelined it for the car.

My mission did not involve Oscar yet.

Once in the car, I fumbled around in the inside zipper pocket of my backpack. When I'd been cleaning up the scattered beer cans in Dad's bedroom, I'd found this small, hand-carved wooden box. It wasn't hidden; it was just underneath his side of the bed. I'd known what it was before I'd opened it: his stash of weed. There wasn't much, maybe enough to pack his Rasta-colored glass bowl—which was also in the box—two or three times.

I stared at the box on my lap and then scanned the hospice parking lot. Not a soul. Before "probation brain" got hold of me, I packed the bowl and took a hit. I smoked, not because I had to, but because I wanted to. Mostly because it was Dad's pot.

When Dad landed in the hospice and the doctor explained that he wouldn't be coming home, that he would die in that room, in that bed, I made a plan to smoke a hit when he had a day left. Today was that day. Now was the time.

I figured, Dad was a rebel. Always was. And he'd die one. The toke-up was in his honor, to let him know that I understood him and that I'd never forget how he'd lived his life—with freedom, with a fierceness. Like every human being, I'm sure he had regrets, but he didn't let them box him up. He powered onward.

Me taking a hit was powering onward.

I closed my eyes, and instead of going ahead in time, I went back, back to his last morning awake. I'd gone in to say goodbye to him before I left for school and found him sitting up in bed, staring out the window. "I'm heading out, Dad. Don't forget you have your liver doctor appointment when we get home. Four thirty. Shower up, okay? You need one."

He saluted me. "All right, *Dad*."

I shoved his foot and laughed.

"Have a good day at school, Vance."

I saluted him back.

The fact that the last time we talked wasn't awful or full of anger was so great. Maybe the greatest thing of all.

Oscar crossed the parking lot. He was about to pass me when I slid my window down.

He scowled. "I thought you weren't allowed to smoke weed anymore."

"Get in," I said. Discussing my motivation for smoking wasn't his business.

Oscar glared at me.

"It's serious. Get in," I said.

"Is it Dad?"

"I'm not telling you shit until you get in." I slid my window closed.

He huffed, walked around the front of the car, and got in.

I gripped the steering wheel. "His breathing is down to four breaths a minute."

"How do you know?"

I exhaled. "How the hell do you think I know? I was just up there."

"Did she say how much time he has left?"

"A day, maybe less." I couldn't look at him when I said it. I didn't want to see the news register on his face. My gaze was straight ahead. A red sports car drove by.

"I'm going back up," Oscar said. He jogged to the front door and disappeared inside the building.

As I put the wooden box away, zipping it inside the pocket, the last thing I'd said in my dad's ear up there went through my head: *You gotta wake up, man. We leave for Jamaica in a few months. Seriously.* If Oscar hadn't been listening to his music and he'd heard me say it, no doubt he would've thought I was a clueless idiot asking Dad to wake up.

I wasn't an idiot.

I knew he wasn't waking up. But I didn't know if he was afraid, if he knew that he was dying. I thought if I talked to him as if he were just sleeping, as if he *could* wake up, then maybe he wouldn't be afraid. The logic was shaky, yes, but when your dad was about to die, crazy shit started making sense.

OSCAR

Vance and I decide not to wear suits to the funeral parlor. We actually share a laugh in the hallway thinking about Dad making fun of us if we wore them. *He* wasn't even wearing one in his casket. One of Ms. Becker's questions for us was what we wanted to have Dad wear. I remember Vance and I looked at each other and said, "Not a suit."

Vance is still puttering around in the kitchen. I sit on the edge of my bed and continue wrestling with the same question: *Should I put one of my sketches in the casket with him?*

When Vance said he wanted to play the song for him, I'd leaned toward "Yes, I should put a sketch in," but now that we're about to leave and the whole thing is about to happen, I am unsure.

Would he want one of my sketches in with him for all eternity? He'd never seen one when he was alive—which has tortured me since leaving the hospice—so would he even *like* what I draw? The sheet is soft under my palms as I run my hands back and forth.

Maybe the gesture is for me, the living. Maybe Dad wouldn't care one way or another. Having such an intimate part of me, such a secret and private part of me, tucked inside with him could be a small comfort...for me.

I reach for my sketchbook and thumb through.

"You ready? We should head out," Vance shouts up the steps.

My heart knocks in my chest. "Be right down." The decision of which drawing was made long ago. I flip right to the page. It's Dad behind the bar at the Blue Mountain. There's only one man sitting having a drink. Dad's head is tossed back and he's laughing. He didn't see me come in that day. I wasn't supposed to work but I hadn't felt like going home. I'd planned to just sit at one of the tables on the restaurant side and do my homework. After a while, it became clear to me that no one knew I was there, so I started drawing.

I carefully tear it out along the perforated edge and hold it up. It's folded and in my back pocket by the time I reach the

K. M. Walton

bottom step. "I feel like we brought stuff to Mom's. Are we forgetting things?" I ask.

Vance's face scrunches. "We are. The zoo photo." He heads into the living room to grab it. He holds it up, shouts, "Got it," and high-fives me as he passes. The sharp smack of his palm on mine is jolting. We haven't high-fived since we were kids. I was always jealous watching Vance and Dad share excitement like that. Hungry for someone, anyone to be happy to see me. And now my brother...*my brother*...is treating me like a friend.

I am not alone anymore.

I smile. "That T-shirt looks good on you." He had on Dad's beloved vintage Jamaican Red Stripe. Dad had been wearing it that day I'd sketched him laughing behind the bar. The T-shirt was faded yellow with a drawn beer cap in the middle of the chest. Across the top of the cap it said "Jamaica's" in bold red script, and then in the center, it had a thick red stripe that ran diagonally with the words "Red Stripe" across it. In the bottom right of the cap, it said in block print "Lager Beer."

After hanging up with Ms. Becker yesterday, Vance and I picked out what Dad would wear. Vance came up with the idea of us each wearing one of his favorite T-shirts. It was the best idea my brother ever had, and I told him so.

Vance looked down and rubbed his chest. "You don't think this is the one we should've had *him* wear, do you?"

"No way. His Blue Mountain Lounge was his favorite."

"You're right." Vance blew out his breath. "Dad would totally approve of that chili stain on yours." He pointed to the center of my chest.

"That's why I picked this one." I'd chosen Dad's Jamaican sunset silk-screen T-shirt that he'd bought from one of the West Chester artisans in town. He said he'd bought it at the very first West Chester Chili Festival, worn it, spilled chili on it, and then two days later I was born. The story, now that he's gone, has taken on a different meaning for me. My father lived his life, stains and all.

I used to get angry with him for wearing this grubby, old, stained T-shirt. He would always tell me to lighten up.

Choosing this shirt is part of my plan to lighten up.

VANCE

YESTERDAY

Oscar held his hand just over Dad's mouth to check for breath.

"Do you feel anything?" I asked.

His eyes bulged. "N-no." Oscar lost it.

My legs refused to hold me up. I fell backward into the chair. *Oh my God.* I wasn't ready for him to go yet! He couldn't be gone. I dropped my head into my hands. "Oh my God. Oh my God."

Images and memories flashed in my brain: Dad pushing me down a snowy hill on my teal-blue saucer sled, him and Mom holding hands at the zoo, his bright-red face when he forgot to reapply sunscreen during the family trip to Jamaica, the way his shoulders popped when a good reggae song came on at the bar, the way he walked, talked, laughed, smiled.

I raised my eyes just as Oscar was trying to move Dad's head. *Were people supposed to handle the dead right after they died?* It didn't seem right to me. He shouldn't touch him. I barked, "What are you doing? S-stop! Stop! Don't touch him!"

Oscar immediately dropped Dad's hand, and his limp arm fell like a tree trunk. *No! That's not right either.* Just then, at that exact moment, there was a knock on the door. Oscar and I turned, and in walked Jacque Beaufort. There wasn't time for me to wipe off my tears and runny nose. I didn't want her in here. This was none of her business. I yelled, "Not now!"

She jumped back a step and apologized. Without another second of hesitation, she turned and ran out.

She was lucky I didn't throw anything at her. A powerful surge of anger shot through my body like a million pistols unloading their bullets. *He should not be dead! How can he be dead? Oh my God.* Dad and I understood each other, we accepted each other. No one, not even Growler, would ever be able to come close to him. *Dad, come back!* Without thinking, I punched the seat of the chair. I had to try to get some of the anger out. My body temperature went through the roof. Beads of sweat ran down my temples.

I needed my fist to land on something again. The chair got it. Unintelligible sounds accompanied each punch. I sounded like an angry bear.

"Vance? Vance!" someone shouted.

I froze mid-punch and raised my eyes. I had to blink rapidly to clear away the tears. Peggy stood a few feet away, and she didn't look happy. "You can either dig deep and calm yourself down, or I can call down to Thomas and he can help you calm down." Peggy turned to Oscar. "Thomas is six-five and three hundred pounds."

Freaking out while sandwiched between Dad's bed and the chair wasn't something I'd planned on. It just came over me. I did not want to meet Thomas.

Like an imploding building, I fell to my knees. The crook of my arm captured my sobs. Peggy sat in the chair I'd just been beating the shit out of and whispered, "If you are hurting deeply, it's because you loved him deeply."

That made me pause. And then a crapload of questions attacked me rapid fire: Why does this nurse have to be named after my mom? Why did my mom have to die? Will Dad finally get to apologize to her? How can I have no living parents? Who will call us down on Christmas morning? What will we do with all of Dad's things? Am I old enough to take over the Blue Mountain? How will I call my grandparents without knowing the phone number? Where is Oscar going?

Oscar walked out. Peggy said, "Let's get you off the floor, hon." I politely refused her help and got myself into the chair. She said she'd let me have some privacy. Once I was alone, I rested my forehead on the mattress and continued crying like a baby.

I felt stupid talking out loud. He wasn't there anymore. *Did I say goodbye?* My head throbbed. I didn't know if I'd said goodbye. With panic in my voice I stuttered, "G-goodbye, Dad. I love you." That wasn't enough. I had more to say. "I will make you proud. You'll see."

OSCAR

SINCE DAD'S SERVICE IS PRIVATE, THE FUNERAL DIREC-
tor leads me and Vance directly to the room where he's laid
out. We pass by the large room where Mom had been laid out.
I shudder. Vance looks away.

With Mom, I remember the three of us in a small room
in the back. We were given some private time with her before
they brought her into the big room. It was in that room that
I popped one of Mom's antianxiety pills. My choice was, take
it or not be there for her viewing. I'd been dangerously close
to passing out ever since I'd woken up that day. Sometimes I
regret not being completely aware that night. Other times I'm
thankful I was at least physically there. I'll never be at peace
with it.

The funeral director is a somber, yet kind guy. He's really tall and completely gray. I'm wondering the same thing as the last time I saw him: How does he get his dress shoes so shiny? He opens the door to a much smaller version of the room Mom was in. Besides the baby-blue tone of the room, I don't notice anything but Dad's open coffin.

The shiny-shoed man walks us in, and we stop about five feet away. "If you'd like to place anything in the casket with your father, boys, you don't need permission. Just go ahead and put it in there."

Vance walks up to Dad and lays the family photo near his head. I nod to the guy, and he asks how much time we'd like before allowing our guests to come back. Hearing him say "our guests" causes a jolt of anxiety. I thought it was just Joey and Bill. I can't handle anyone else. "Just Joey McSweeny and Bill Peterson, right?"

"That's still up to you gentlemen. More are welcome, if need be," he says.

Vance turns around. "No, just those two."

"As you wish," he says. "I'll close the door on my way out, but my office is right across the hall when you're ready." He does as he says and gently pulls the door shut.

"He doesn't look that bad," Vance says.

I crinkle my face.

Vance responds to my cringe. "His skin looks healthier now than when he was alive at the end. Come look. I'm serious."

We stand shoulder to shoulder and gaze upon our father's body. He actually *doesn't* look as bad as he did in the hospice. "You're right."

"Right?" he echoes. After we silently stare at Dad, out of the blue Vance blurts out, "Do you think Mom crashed into the tree on purpose?"

That question was something I'd toyed with after she was gone. "No, I don't. She'd never have left you and me on purpose. It was an accident."

"But you weren't there during their last fight. It was brutal." Vance's voice is a whisper. "What if he pushed her to the edge?"

I look at my brother as his layers fall to the floor.

"He *did* push her to the edge, Vance. But she didn't jump. I know it right here." I pat my heart. "She lost control of her car by accident."

Vance turns away and cries into his bent arm. I wonder what Dad must think of us, standing over his body discussing the possibility of Mom committing suicide because of him. It's not right.

With his back still to me, Vance says, "I've been wrestling with that question since her burial. Probably thought about it a thousand times—I don't know, maybe more. I wish I'd asked you a long time ago."

When he faces me, I nod. Words seem like too much right now.

Again we stand side by side, grasping the side of Dad's casket. My brain drowns as I reminiscence about moments from my childhood, small moments—Dad putting a Band-Aid on my knee after my bike wipeout, Mom quizzing me with math flash cards, the Christmas morning I had a fever. Each memory slices my heart. I close my eyes.

Love is the emotion that rips you up memory by memory.

The statement tumbles around, bumping into everything, and I'm laser-focused on the word "love." My mother's love was never in question; it was always Dad's. There was no doubt that he failed to understand me, never took the time to, but his love...

I study his body, starting at the hands. Flashes of him pop—him bustling around behind the bar, making drinks, pulling beers, working hard.

Working hard.

Working hard.

Working hard.

The words repeat.

Dad worked hard for me, for Vance. Our bursting college

funds are proof. Our house, clothes, food, all additional evidence. Maybe providing was how he loved me. Instead of telling me, he showed me, subtly. The words were always buried for him. It was complicated.

I don't want my memories to shred me. They need to hold me together. This, I believe, is within my control. It has to be.

I stand up straight and force myself to be present. Vance is right. Dad's skin does look better. But unlike Mom, who looked as if she was going to sit up any minute, *he'd* lost a lot of weight since his accident and his hair was thin and patchy. Ms. Becker had called yesterday with a question from the mortician who wanted permission to give Dad a haircut. Vance and I had looked at each other and shrugged. I told Ms. Becker that was fine.

So his hair is nice and tight to his head. No one would ever know he had lost so much just before he died.

"The haircut was a good move," Vance says.

A warm tear glides down my cheek.

"Should I play the song?" he asks.

I nod.

Vance pulls out his phone. He taps the screen until the soft organ sounds that open "Many Rivers to Cross" float into our ears. We look at each other, both with dripping, broken faces. He lowers the phone and holds it to Dad's ear just as Jimmy

Cliff's haunting voice sings. Without qualms, I put my arm around Vance's shoulder. He tosses his around mine.

We choke on our sobs. We squeeze each other's shoulders. We listen as Jimmy Cliff serenades our dead father.

We do all these things together. As brothers. Finally, finally as brothers.

I am not alone.

Vance and I pull into our driveway. Jacque Beaufort is sitting on our back steps. She stands and gives us a little wave.

Vance turns to me. "Did you invite her here?"

"No," I say, my face no doubt drained of color.

"Shit. I don't have it in me to talk to anyone."

My feelings are identical, but it is Jacque Beaufort, and she is standing in my yard. "I'll talk to her."

"Cool. Thanks." He accepts a hug from her and then excuses himself.

"Hey," I say.

"Hi." She tucks her hair and rests her hands on her neck. "I went to the funeral home, but they said the service was private so I came here and waited. I'm so sorry, Oscar."

"Thank you." The fact that she made the effort to go to Dad's service makes my heart swell. That gesture is like a spotlight on *her* kind heart. And she's here, in the dark, waiting for me.

My brain could detonate with these facts.

"How are you doing?" she asks. Before I can respond with *awful, shitty, destroyed,* she smacks her forehead. "Stupid question, Oscar. Sorry."

"It's okay." My brain is short-circuiting with pain and confusion, shock and longing.

She holds out her arms, and without hesitation I walk into her embrace. It's warm and perfect. She squeezes me tight and rubs my back. "I'm just so sorry." We stand, wrapped up in each other, for what feels like centuries, each second full of exactly what I need: acceptance.

Jacque gently kisses my cheek before pulling away. "I'm here when you need me."

My knees buckle as I step back. Jacque Beaufort just kissed me. I want to rub my face, but that would be weird so I stand like a statue instead. Equally as odd, certainly.

I nod and whisper another thank-you.

It's like she knows not to push me to talk. "Go see if you can get some sleep. I'm sure you guys are wiped out." She heads down the driveway, turning back once she reaches the sidewalk, and we lock eyes.

Jacque has never looked more beautiful to me.

VANCE

TWO MONTHS LATER

I glanced at Oscar's sketch of Dad—the one he did in the hospice, the one I gave him so much shit over. Unbeknownst to him I made a photocopy of it. I carefully folded it up into a square and tucked it inside my graduation cap.

A few days after Dad's burial, Oscar brought out his sketchbook at the dinner table. He had never done that before. He asked if there was a particular drawing that I liked, one that "spoke to me." I'd raised my eyebrows and asked him to explain what "spoke to me" meant. He did, and I knew exactly which drawing. The one he drew of Mom on the phone. He nodded and said, "Yeah, that one is my favorite too."

When we were clearing the dishes, he asked if there was another one that I liked.

Without a pause I'd said, "The one you did of Dad in the hospice."

"Really? The one you gave me shit over? *That* one?" He was busting my balls.

I'd dropped my chin and mumbled, "Yeah, *that* one." Me flipping out on Oscar was stupid. Thinking back, it didn't even make sense. What was the big deal about him drawing Dad? I didn't have a logical reason. It was more like I'd been scared shitless and my brother took the brunt of my raging fear.

"Surprising. I thought you'd have picked one of you with Dad."

I'd surprised myself actually. The ones with me and Dad were great, but it was the nakedness of his face in the hospice sketch, the way Oscar was able to almost capture his soul. "It was beautiful and terrible at the same time."

Oscar looked me dead in the eye. "You saw that?" he'd whispered.

A few days later, when I woke up, the drawing sat on my dresser with a note from Oscar.

Dear Vance,

I know graduation will be emotionally confusing—joy __and__ aching sadness. So I'm giving you the sketch of Dad from the hospice. Yes, I realize it's a somber drawing, but like I said, the day won't be all one thing. I wanted you to have something that represented those complicated emotions. As ~~you~~ said before, the drawing was "beautiful and terrible at the same time."

You'll never know how much it means to me to have you respect my artwork. I always thought you and Dad would make fun of me for it. So to have you tell me—to my face—that you think I'm good means everything to me.

Oscar

I zipped up my graduation gown, placed the cap on my head, and stared at myself in the mirror. The edge of the folded drawing poked into my head. I was okay with that. In fact, I liked it. It would be the perfect reminder that Oscar's drawing was there. That *Dad* was there. I also wore Mom's wedding ring on a silver chain around my neck. That was my brother's brilliant idea. And it allowed me to keep Mom's plastic ziplock bag in my drawer, sealed and private. Maybe I'd tell Oscar one day. Maybe I wouldn't.

I removed the drawing from my cap and tossed it into the big, brown envelope. I would put it back later. I had a surprise for Oscar.

"We should go, Vance!" Oscar shouted from downstairs.

I patted my heart. "Here we go, Mom and Dad."

We were in the car about to back up when I handed Oscar the envelope.

"What's this?" He held it up.

I hadn't planned on surprising him until after graduation, but I couldn't wait. "Check out the paper-clipped stuff first."

Oscar unclasped the envelope and pulled out the papers. He flipped through and looked over with wide eyes. "Dad never canceled it?"

"Nope." A few weeks before Dad's accident, I was about to knock on his office door, but when I heard the words, "Yes, the boys have their passports," I dropped my arm and eavesdropped. He was on the phone with the travel agent. He never did cancel our trip to Jamaica, and by what I heard, we were still going. Hearing that news lifted my heart so high it felt like it might burst through the top of my head. Dad was obviously going to surprise *me*. He didn't hate me.

"So we're really going?" Oscar sounded unsure. "Am I allowed to?"

I laughed. "Yeah, we're really going. Everything's done and paid for. We already have our passports. And who's going to stop us? I'm your guardian, remember?"

Oscar dropped his head. For a second I thought he was upset, but then he smiled and snorted. "Dad would definitely want us to go."

He went to put the envelope underneath his leg. "Wait," I said. "There's something else in there."

Oscar reached in and pulled out his folded drawing. Once it was opened up, he just stared at it. At least a minute passed and then he said, "I don't understand."

I said. "First, don't be mad that it's folded. It's not your original. I made a copy. I'm going to fold it and wear it underneath my cap so Dad's with me today. You cool with that?"

Oscar turned and looked out the window.

Why wasn't he saying anything? "Are you mad?"

"Not mad. Just drive. Give me a minute."

I continued backing out of the driveway. When we were halfway to school, I said, "You all right?"

He took a big, loud breath. "Four months ago, if someone told me that my brother, Vance, was going to fold up one of my sketches and wear it underneath his graduation cap,

I would've fallen on the floor laughing." Oscar smacked his thighs and blew out his breath. "So, what you said to me at the hospice, when we were meeting with Ms. Becker after Dad died. You said we had an ultimatum. Remember?"

I nodded.

"I'd never looked at our situation like that. So black and white. Sometimes I can complicate things."

I laughed. "Yeah, no shit."

"I always thought you and Dad were masters at assuming things. I used to tell myself that all the time. Maybe it was all of us. Maybe we all assumed a whole bunch of stuff about each other. We did, didn't we?"

A red light loomed ahead, and I slowed to a stop. "You're right. It was all of us. All three of us let it get so messed up. Assumptions definitely were part of the problem." The light turned green, and we quietly motored along for a while, lost in our heads. Then it hit me. "You know what? It's simple. Either we're brothers or we're not. And I mean we act like it. We owe it to Mom and Dad to take care of each other."

"I think we're doing it, Vance." Oscar held up his palm and I high-fived him. If hands smacking together could feel like a promise, well, then we just sealed the deal.

I shoved his shoulder. "Of course we're doing it, dipshit. Look at us."

We laughed so hard I nearly missed the next light.

We scored a pretty decent parking spot and walked through the lot. "Is Jacque meeting you at the entrance?" I asked. I'd had a feeling Jacque was there to see Oscar the night of Dad's service. I could tell by the way she kept looking past me, searching for my brother. And about a week later she sent us each our own sympathy card. When Oscar's face went purple after reading his, I was sure his note was more than what I got:

I'm so sorry for your loss, Vance.

Sincerely,
Jacque Beaufort.

"What did she write to *you*?" I'd asked him. My normally private brother handed me the card.

Dear Oscar,

First let me say how incredibly brokenhearted I am for your loss. I can't even imagine the pain you must be in. Please know that I think of you a lot. Anyway, I hope you finish out the school year. Being in the busy halls of WCHS could be a good distraction. But if you decide to do cyber school or something, that's cool. I meant what I said in your yard that night—I'm here if you need me. I know now is not the time to make plans so I'll text you in a few days or weeks. I'm not sure how long I should wait. Maybe you can text me when you're ready to talk?

With <u>all</u> my sympathy,
Jacque Beaufort

PS Remember when I was all blabby that day at the piano, going all deep? I've always thought <u>you</u> had a quiet confidence like my mom. I could tell you had a lot going on underneath the surface. That intrigued me. Oh, and you're a really excellent hugger.

"Holy shit, dude. She likes you," I'd said.

Oscar shook his head. "I don't know what to do. *You're* the one with all the experience with girls."

The moment was huge. I'd felt the weight of it on my shoulders. Oscar only had me to talk to. Only me. I held out my hand and said, "Can we make a pact that we're not going to repeat the mistakes Dad made with Mom?"

Oscar squinted before grasping my hand. "Yeah, sure. But, I thought you wanted to be just like Dad."

I'd sat on the sofa and motioned for him to do the same. "When Mom was still alive, I used to think that was how it was supposed to be, that guys couldn't be faithful." I shook my head. "But after my accident, things changed for me. It was like I saw everything differently. Dad treated her like shit. She wasn't happy. I saw it in her eyes in your drawing. I saw it in her eyes in *real life*. And Dad definitely wasn't happy. I think all the drinking he did after she died was his guilt. Deep down, I think he knew he fucked up."

Oscar held his fists next to his temples and then fanned his hands out wide. "Mind. Blown."

"I feel things too. Wild, eh?"

We'd sat till ten o'clock talking. Another first for us. I'd even walked him through what to text Jacque and where to go on their first date—the Black Bean coffee shop in town.

They've been inseparable ever since.

I pulled my cap down a little as I neared the gym doors. Oscar still hadn't answered me. "Hellooo? Is Jacque meeting you before she goes in?" She was graduating today too.

Oscar stared through me. I snapped in front of his face. "Sorry," he said. "Yes. She's meeting me right here."

"Vance, before *you* go in, what I love about classical music is that it's complex. The way it let me escape to a place where I could just *be*. It's the way it allowed me to remain introverted but all the while challenging me with its aesthetic lure—"

I grabbed his shoulders. "Dude, you said you were going to

stop talking like that. Remember? And you're not making any sense. I gotta go. Cheer loud when they call my name, okay?"

Oscar returned the gesture and clasped my forearms. "Wait. I have a point. *I'm* complex. You're simple. And I don't mean that as an insult. I'm the ying to your yang. We complement each other. Down. Up. Ying. Yang."

I smiled and gave his shoulders a squeeze. "Whatever you say, buddy."

"I know what I want now."

His eyes were glassy. Crap, *I* didn't want to walk in there crying. *He knows what he wants? Huh?* "Can we talk about it afterward?"

"What you owe me, remember? For breaking the news to Dad for you? I finally know what I want. The hatchet that we've carried around since childhood, I'd like it buried. Underneath concrete."

Oscar extended his hand and I grasped it. After a few shakes, I pulled him in for a hug and we smacked each other's backs. "Look at us. We're doing it again."

ACKNOWLEDGMENTS

To my husband and sons—Todd, Christian, and Jack—you three are my magic.

To my first readers, Mary Anne Becker-Sheedy, Todd Walton, and Christian Walton, thank you for your fervent belief in me and my writing—it does a stellar job of silencing the doubt monster.

To my critique partners, Elisa Ludwig and Christina Lee, your discerning feedback was beyond helpful while shaping this book, thank you. I am a lucky author.

To my agent, Jim McCarthy, thank you for adopting me with such graciousness and verve and for alllllll of your hard work.

To my editor, Annette Pollert-Morgan, your keen eye continues to push and enrich my writing, and for that I will be eternally grateful.

To my sister, Nikole Becker, who, like in *Cracked*, is once again an actual character. The amazing character Ms. Becker is solidly based on her. She is an incredible social worker with an incredible heart.

To my mom, stepfather, sisters, brother-in-laws, nieces, nephews, aunts, uncles, and in-laws, thank you for loving me, thank you for supporting me with abandon, thank you for being the best family on earth.

To my COUSINS! COUSINS!, Joe, Kathleen, Lisa, Susan, Francine, Jennifer, Michael C., Robert, Chris, Patty, Colleen, Maureen, Genny, Jimmy, Joe P., Michael M., Jacque, Mike H., Annemarie, Michael M., Morgan, and the late John, I am so blessed to be part of the McGettigan legacy. Thank you for the lifetime of love, friendship, SUPPORT, laughter, and dancing.

Thank you to the team at Sourcebooks for all your hard work behind the scenes. What a brilliant village!

To my dedicated and passionate readers, I drop infinity thank-yous at your feet.

ABOUT THE AUTHOR

K. M. Walton is the author of *Cracked* and *Empty*. Mean people baffle her—she's so passionate about acceptance that she gives school presentations titled "The Power of Human Kindness." K. M. lives in Pennsylvania with her husband, two sons, and cat. Visit the author at kmwalton.com.